He cupped her face in his hands and lowered his mouth to hers.

The touch was meant to be sweet and tender but quickly turned hot and demanding. Sam traced her lips with his tongue and Faith opened to him. She settled her hands on his chest, pressing closer, and he slid an arm around her waist, holding her tighter.

The sound of their breathing filled his ears, drowning out the night sounds. He wanted her and she wanted him right back. But… There was that damn word again.

He lifted his head. "Faith, we can't— There's a—"

"Wedding reception," she said, her voice barely a whisper.

"Yeah." He stepped away from temptation and willed her to believe what he was going to say. "You should know this isn't sudden—kissing you, I mean."

"I know. It wasn't for me either."

"I've wanted to do that for a while."

"I can't say I haven't wanted you to."

"Okay, then." He blew out a long breath. "Fair warning. At an appropriate time, there will be more kissing. And stuff. Unless you're not interested. I'll back off. Just say the word and—"

She shook her head. "I'm all in favor of…stuff."

"Good."

"It's love I have a problem with."

So did he. How perfect was that?

* * *

The Bachelors Of Blackwater Lake:
They won't be single for long!

THE NEW GUY IN TOWN

BY
TERESA SOUTHWICK

First Published in Great Britain 2017
By Mills & Boon, an imprint of HarperCollins*Publishers*
1 London Bridge Street, London, SE1 9GF

ISBN: 978-0-263-92308-7

23-0617

Our policy is to use papers that are natural, renewable and recyclable products and made from wood grown in sustainable forests. The logging and manufacturing processes conform to the legal environmental regulations of the country of origin.

Printed and bound in Spain
by CPI, Barcelona

Teresa Southwick lives with her husband in Las Vegas, the city that reinvents itself every day. An avid fan of romance novels, she is delighted to be living out her dream of writing for Mills & Boon.

To my father, Frank Boyle.
I learned to love reading and writing from you,
and the lessons were priceless.
Miss you, Dad.

Chapter One

Just because she'd sworn off men didn't mean she couldn't appreciate a gorgeous one. That explained Faith Connelly's little heart flutter as Sam Hart walked briskly across the elegant lobby of his financial building before stopping in front of her flower cart.

"Don't tell me," she said to him. "You need to order a breakup bouquet. I can tell by the look on your face that date number two tanked."

"That's harsh." But Sam smiled a slow, sexy smile that said she was right and the date from hell was completely his fault. He wore his willingness to own the blame like a badge of honor. "And how can you know that? Maybe I'm here to tell you that it was love at first sight."

"Right." She made a scoffing sound. "And I kissed a frog into a handsome prince. Seriously, Sam, do you want the usual sentiment on the card? 'You're fantastic, but this isn't going to work.' Or there's the ever-popular 'It's not you, it's me.' I can get more creative with the message if you'd like."

He slid his fingers into the pockets of his jeans. He could wear jeans to work because he owned a multimillion-dollar financial company and set the dress code. Sometimes he wore a suit and that was a swoon-worthy look, too. "Give me a for instance."

She thought for a moment then met his skeptical gaze. "How about this? It's short, sweet, to the point and kind of poetic really. 'Roses are red. Violets are blue. This won't work because you're a shrew.'"

His mouth twitched, then he shook his head and laughed. When he did that he was so handsome it should be illegal. His brown hair was cut short, but there were hints that it would be curly if allowed to grow. The straight nose and square jaw alone would have women throwing their panties at him, but it was his eyes that sealed the deal. They were dark blue and full of glitter and sin and danger—if a girl wasn't careful.

"Don't give up your day job to write inspirational verses for greeting cards," he said.

"The thought never crossed my mind. I love working with the flowers. And another perk of my job is torturing you about your women."

"My women?" He put on an innocent act, pretending indignation. "You make me sound like the pharaoh with forty-seven wives."

"If the shoe fits…" She was teasing. Mostly.

Since he'd moved to Blackwater Lake, Montana a few months ago, Sam Hart had quickly become a hot topic of gossip. Because he was definitely hot, and that made the gossip juicier. His looks weren't all women noticed, though that lean, athletic body made more than one female heart skip a beat. When you factored in his impressive net worth as a member of the wealthy Hart family, attention from the opposite sex looking for love—or just a wealthy husband—was a fact of life. It was a dirty job, but someone had to be the town's most eligible bachelor.

His expression turned adorably self-effacing and wounded. "You have no faith in me, Faith."

"Really?" She tsked. "How long have you been trying to work that into a conversation with me?"

"Probably since we met." He shrugged his broad shoulders. "But here's the thing—I like women and they seem to like me. You're judging, Miss Connelly, and not in a good way. I'm picking up shades of assumption from you. Why is that? I'm a swell guy."

"If you're trying to seduce me, Sam, I should probably tell you that it's not working." And never would.

"Darn." He snapped his fingers. "How can you be so sure?"

Besides the fact that she believed love was a four-letter word, the bad kind, she knew he was a player. "Seriously? No one knows you better than the plant lady."

"You do have a way with flowers," he said, looking all meek and faux innocent.

"And you have a way with women. That makes you one of my best customers." She held up her fingers to count the ways. "A single yellow rose on the first date to indicate sunny feelings, warmth and welcome. The color holds no overtones of romance and indicates purely platonic emotions."

"So you told me." There was amusement in those blue eyes. "And you were right. It's a crowd-pleaser."

"The second date you buy a mixed bouquet so there's no hint of commitment. If things don't go well, there will be a lovely and tasteful arrangement to let a lady know not to wait by the phone for a call that will never come." She met his gaze. "FYI, I always use peonies in the arrangement to indicate their indignation and your shame."

"Do you put that on the card?"

"It's enough that I know the significance," she said.

"I'll keep that in mind." He frowned slightly. "And you see this flower fetish of mine as a flaw?"

"On the contrary. It's a public service. A woman always knows where she stands with you."

"Just out of curiosity, what's the appropriate bloom to offer on a third date?" he asked.

"Good question. I'd have to do some research. But never, under any circumstances, go with lavender. It conveys enchantment, as in love at first sight." Faith studied him again. "Why are you asking about a third date? Do you want to give me breaking news? Is there something I should know? Maybe someone who has snagged a cherished and sought-after third-time's-the-charm date with the elusive Sam Hart? Do I need an inventory change? Possibly to get ready for a wedding?"

"God forbid. Why would you say that?"

"Because a third date with you almost never happens, Sam."

"That can't be true." His expression turned thoughtful, obviously trying to come up with something to prove her wrong, and then he sighed. "Am I that predictable?"

"Sadly, yes," she said smugly.

"Wow. Remind me to change things up."

"Not on my account. If you ever settle down, my bottom line will seriously suffer. A money guy like you should understand that." She leveled her index finger in his direction to emphasize her point. "And I can't afford to jeopardize my revenue stream while saving to put Phoebe through college."

"Your daughter is eight." His voice was wry. "You've got ten years."

"A single mom has to plan carefully." Because thanks to

her bastard ex-husband, who walked out on her when she got pregnant, she was raising her daughter alone.

"Well, never fear, plant lady. I'm not getting married." His devil-may-care air slipped, a tell that he would only commit to dodging a trip down the aisle.

"That sounds fairly adamant."

"Because it is," he confirmed.

"Don't worry. I'll keep your secret. If the single women of Blackwater Lake found out they have no chance to win your affections, it could cramp your style." Although women had a bad habit of believing they could be the one to change a man's mind. Faith wasn't one of them, however. "And your style is going to pad my daughter's education fund."

"It's good to know that professional confidentiality is for lawyers, doctors and florists."

His blunt admission fertilized her curiosity about his aversion to matrimony but the whys of it were a conversation for another day. "So where should I deliver the breakup bouquet?"

"I haven't confirmed I'm ordering one." He stopped as something occurred to him. "Do you really call it that?"

"Of course. I could do a whole marketing campaign on it thanks to you."

"Ouch."

"I'm not making fun of you—"

"Yes," he said. "You are."

"Okay, I am." She grinned. "But I do it with a great deal of affection." And a fair amount of flirting.

Her inner flirt had been in permanent time-out until she'd met Sam Hart. He was a walking, talking warning about why she'd sworn off men. Lack of commitment. Flitting from one woman to the next. Pretty to look at but shallow as a cookie sheet. The silver lining was that the reminder came with built-in caution to never let her interaction with him be more than business. Hence, he was safe to flirt with.

"Okay, then, at the risk of making you even more insufferable than you already are, I'd like to send a lovely, tasteful bouquet. With peonies," he added.

It was really hard not to gloat. But she was nothing if not a plant professional. "Where would you like it delivered? And what's the name on the card?"

"Blackwater Lake Lodge—"

"Ah. A tourist."

"Really?" His tone scolded her.

"Not judging," she said quickly. "Just an observation. A name would be helpful."

He hesitated for a moment, then sighed. "Kiki Daniels. And don't you dare—"

"Never crossed my mind," she lied, pressing her lips together to suppress a smile or any words that might try to slip out.

"I don't believe you." He gave her the room number and instructed her to put it on the credit card she had on file for him. "You're dying to say something so spit it out before you explode."

"Okay. Does she look like a Kiki? I mean perky and—" she held her hands out in front of her chest "—lots of personality? Long blond hair and flaky as a French pastry?"

"Wow," he said. "Stereotype much?"

"It's just that I know you so it's not exactly stereotyping." She had an order pad and pen ready. "What do you want the card to say?"

He thought for a moment. "'It's been fun. Best of luck.' Sign it Sam."

"Past tense and positive. Got it." She jotted down the words. "I'll take care of this for you. Anything else?"

"Yes, actually. My parents are in town and it's my mother's

birthday. I've put off shopping because the woman has everything." He dragged his fingers through his hair.

"I can do a beautiful arrangement. What's her favorite color?"

He stared at her for several moments. "I didn't know there would be a pop quiz. And don't even think about asking what her favorite flower is."

"What kind of a son are you? How can you not know your mother's favorite color?" She was teasing.

"Hold that thought." He pulled out his cell phone and hit speed dial. A moment later he said, "Ellie, I need some information. Okay. You're right. That was abrupt. Hi, how are you?" There was an impatient look on his face as he listened. "Glad to hear it. What's mom's favorite color and flower?" He nodded. "Got it. Thanks. See you tonight at dinner." He met her gaze. "Star lilies. And pink."

"Excellent. Pink ribbon it is." She wrote down his sister's address which was where his parents were staying. "I'll go back to the store and put together something very special for her and deliver it on my way home."

"Thanks, Faith."

"Anything else?" she asked.

"That should do it." He smiled. "You're a lifesaver."

"Anytime. Enjoy your evening."

Faith watched him walk out the building's double glass doors and objectively analyzed the man's butt. On a scale of one to ten his was an eleven and a half, which made her sigh. There was no denying she loved owning her business and working with flowers. The colors and scent of the blooms. Putting different ones together for a colorful and creative effect. Everything.

Then Sam Hart had moved to town and turned into a lucrative account. Work became a lot more interesting, not just from teasing him, but because it gave her a chance to deliver flowers and get a look at the women he rejected.

Somehow it was comforting to know that perfectly pretty women didn't have perfect lives any more than she did.

But it also made her curious. Every woman she'd met so far had been both beautiful and nice, which made her wonder why not even one of them had earned date number three. Someday she was going to find out what was up with that. So sue her—she was female and liked gossip as much as any other female in Blackwater Lake.

A week after his mother's birthday, Sam Hart was talking to his sister on the phone. He leaned back in his office chair and glanced at the paperwork on his desk. The sheer volume was a measure of his success, which should make him happy. *Should* being the operative word. He thought moving closer to Ellie and her family and his brother Linc, who'd recently relocated, would make his restlessness go away. It hadn't.

He loved his work, assessing risk and evaluating financial products for banking customers. Handling commercial and real estate loans. Managing grants for enterprising small business owners. A vision of Faith Connelly popped into his mind and her flower shop—Every Bloomin' Thing.

The pretty plant lady had approached him on his first day in this new building—Hart Financial, LLC. She'd negotiated a price to lease space in the lobby for her flower cart, making the case that his clients might benefit from the convenience. Just limited hours at first because she had to cover her main store in downtown Blackwater Lake.

As office occupancy in the building increased and foot traffic grew, she would hire another employee to work the cart while she took care of the shop. Until then customers would have to deal with her. He smiled, recalling her rhyming *blue* with *shrew.* Not only was she pretty, but she always made him laugh. Since his protracted and ugly divorce he hadn't laughed all that much, so it was noteworthy.

"Sam? Are you listening to me?" The pitch of Ellie's voice sharpened.

"Of course." He hoped there wasn't a test. "You were telling me how much mom liked the birthday flowers."

"'Liked' is an understatement. You get the son-of-the-year award. Possibly a lifetime achievement plaque. Cal sent a gift card and Linc took her to dinner. But she said the star lilies in that bouquet made her day. The scent was magical. In fact, I can still smell them a whole week later."

Sam wasn't about to mention Faith and share the credit. He planned to ride this hero thing as long as it would run. "I'm glad she liked them."

"Not to change the subject, but...have you heard about the fire on Crawford's Crest?"

"Yeah." Sam swiveled his chair and looked out his office window. Clouds of red-tinged black smoke rose from the tree line to the west and curved up the hill. Fortunately it was moving away from town. "Any news on containment?"

"Not that I'm aware of," she admitted. "And this wind is going to make it tough on the firefighters. The last I heard they're calling in reinforcements from all over Montana. Quite a few homes are threatened."

"Looks like it's pretty far away from your place."

"It is," she confirmed. "We're close to the lake and the fire is out near isolated cabins and neighborhoods of older homes at the foot of the mountain."

Sam's new place wasn't far from his sister's so it was safe, too. "Do they know how it started?"

"Lightning ignited dry brush. It's August and there hasn't been much rain. This is a problem every summer."

"The price we pay for the beautiful scenery. And Mother Nature can be a wicked mistress."

"Yeah." She sighed. "Didn't mean to keep you. I just wanted you to know how much Mom enjoyed the flowers while she was here. She asked me to tell you goodbye and that she'll be back to visit soon."

"Thanks for letting me know. I'm glad she liked her birthday gift. Talk to you later, Ellie."

"Love you. Bye."

He hit the end call button and took a last look at the smoke. It was unsettling. Another way one's life could be turned upside down in an instant.

He looked at the paperwork on his desk and sighed. There wasn't anything here that couldn't wait until tomorrow. After shutting down his computer, he left his office on the building's top floor and rode the elevator to the lobby. Faith's cart, with its cheerful sign, Every Bloomin' Thing, and the fragrance of flowers always lifted his spirits.

She was there and he walked over. It looked as if she was packing up for the day. Her long strawberry blond hair was pulled into a messy side bun and long bangs touched her thick eyelashes. Warm brown eyes made her coloring unique and the sprinkle of freckles across her straight nose was pretty cute. She was smart, sassy and every guy's little sister.

Today he didn't have a date and wasn't breaking up with anyone so his only excuse for stopping was to thank her again for her efforts and let her know the bouquet she'd arranged had been a big hit with his mother.

"Hi," he said.

She glanced over her shoulder, then set down the long-stemmed flowers she'd been about to move for transport. "Hi, yourself. Got a hot date tonight?"

"No. Despite what you seem to think, my social life isn't all that active."

"I noticed you've been slacking since your mom came

to visit." She nodded knowingly. "You're smarter than you look."

"Do you talk this way to all your customers?"

"No, actually. Just you."

"Should I feel special?" he asked, not in the least offended.

"If you're not, I didn't do it right."

"So you admit to deliberately provoking me?"

"It's the best part of my day." The words were teasing, but her eyes didn't have their customary impertinence. "Is there something you need?"

"No. I just wanted to let you know my mother loved the birthday arrangement."

"Good." She transferred the flowers to a small hand cart used for moving her inventory from her van to the lobby stand.

"I wanted to thank you. It was a last-minute order and meant keeping you late. The effort is much appreciated."

"You're welcome. If you could give me a Facebook like and say something about my exemplary customer service that would be great."

It flashed through his mind to offer to buy her a drink or dinner as a thank-you but his internal warning system flagged and shut down that thought. He knew the difference between good and bad risk, and an invitation to dinner fell into the really bad column. As the newcomer to Blackwater Lake he was trying to fit in and, as Faith had pointed out more than once, his romantic record was abysmal. Dating and dropping the town sweetheart would not win him the hearts and minds of the locals.

"Are you in a hurry?" It seemed to him that she was distracted while she packed up to go. Now that he thought about it, he was leaving work earlier than usual and normally she was here as he walked out the door, so this was really early for her. "Do *you* have a date?"

"Oh, please…"

He noted the blush that slid into her cheeks. The color reminded him of a pink rose. He recalled the first time he'd bought one and her warning him away from pink or red because the shade symbolized a deepening of feeling. "It's a reasonable question. You're not bad-looking for a smartass."

"Be still, my heart." She rested her hands on the counter between them. "Careful, Sam. Words like that could turn a girl's head."

"That was nothing more than a simple statement of fact. Let me use the rose metaphor to explain."

"Please do." A brief flash of amusement crossed her face.

"Just like you, a rose is beautiful. And then you open your mouth and out come the thorns to jab a guy."

"And yet you keep coming back. Maybe you're a glutton for punishment." Her inner smartass couldn't be silenced for long. "Maybe I should leave the thorns on the first-date roses for you. No pain, no gain. It could work in your favor to get you a third date."

"That twisted logic presupposes I want one."

"That is an intriguing clue into the mystery of Sam Hart. You have no idea how it pains me not to pursue it." She glanced past him to wicked, billowing smoke clearly visible from the tall glass lobby windows. "But you're right. I'm in a hurry, and not because I have a date."

"Then what's so urgent? Is your daughter okay?"

"The fire isn't far from my house. I need to go pack some things for Phoebe and me, just in case we have to evacuate. She's fine," Faith added.

"Good." There was a splash of apprehension in her expression that touched him because it was so different from her usually brazen, audacious behavior. She was every guy's sister and if Ellie's house was in the fire's path he would do anything to keep her safe. "Can I do something to help?"

"Thanks, Sam." She smiled a little. "But I've got it covered."

"What about your daughter?"

"She's at summer camp. Cabot Dixon's ranch. The wind is blowing the fire away from them. He and his wife will keep her until I can pick her up."

"Okay. Then at least let me help you move the flowers back to your store in town. It will be faster," he pointed out.

She wanted to say no. Even a spreadsheet nerd who crunched numbers for a living could see that. But she nodded and said, "Thanks."

Together they got all the flowers on the flat hand cart, then locked up ribbons, tissue paper, cellophane and all the other supplies she kept here. She secured the credit card receipts and cash in her purse, then gave him a nod to head for the exit. Before they took a step, Blackwater Lake's mayor walked into the lobby and straight over to Faith.

Mayor Loretta Goodson-McKnight was an attractive brunette somewhere in her late fifties, but it was asking for trouble to put even a ballpark number on a woman's age. Today she looked a little older and that probably had something to do with the natural disaster she was dealing with. It was her job to coordinate resources and the emergency response. Judging by the expression on her face, whatever she had to say wasn't good.

"Faith, I've got some bad news." The mayor got straight to the point. "We just received word that there's an evacuation order for everyone who lives near Crawford's Crest."

"That's where my house is."

"I know." The woman's voice softened and her expression was sympathetic. "I'm on my way to the staging area right now for an update from the fire captain and wanted to let you know myself."

"And I appreciate it more than you know. I'll just go to the house and grab a few things for us."

The mayor shook her head. "They won't let you through. The sheriff has blocked off the road. You can't go home, honey."

Faith blinked as the meaning of it all sank in and shock took over. "Oh my God. You mean I could really lose it—"

The woman started talking, telling her about everything being done—tankers dropping fire-retardant chemicals and water on the blaze. Firefighters were clearing the brush, trying to deprive the fire of fuel to burn and slow it down so they could surround it. But Sam saw the worry on her face and what she was leaving out. No one could control the wind that was fanning the flames, limiting the ability of ordinary men to save the structures in the fire's path.

"All your neighbors are getting out. That's a lot of people to find shelter for."

Sam watched the color drain from Faith's face and had the most absurd desire to pull her into his arms and tell her everything was going to be fine.

"Faith, honey, we'd rather keep evacuees in private homes as opposed to setting up temporary quarters in the high school gym. You know how people in this town pull together when there's a crisis. My office has lined up volunteers and we've almost got everyone covered. You and Phoebe can stay at my house. It's pretty full, but we have air mattresses and floor space in the living room."

Apparently Sam's male chromosomes, the ones that made him want to fix a problem rather than just stand by and listen, kicked into gear. That was the only explanation for what came out of his mouth. That and the fact that there was no way he would let them sleep on air mattresses, even if it was in the mayor's living room.

He touched Faith's arm. "You and Phoebe can stay with me."

Chapter Two

Faith's sassy inner flirt went absolutely silent and all she could do was stare at Sam for several moments. Then her mind just went numb. "I'm sorry. You want Phoebe and me to do what now?"

"Stay with me." His concern seemed genuine but that didn't mean it was.

Although the look was another winner for him. And the fact that she could even think that in a time of crisis was reason enough to decline the offer. "That's very nice of you. But I wouldn't want to cramp your style."

"What style would that be?"

"You know." She glanced at the mayor, not wanting to discuss his personal life in front of her. Plant lady–client privilege should be as sacred as the confessional.

"No, I don't know." He folded his arms over an impressive chest. The stance oozed challenge, daring her to elaborate.

"Okay then, I'll spell it out. You're a bachelor and you

date a lot. I have a young daughter. It might not be the best arrangement for us."

"As you know, I don't have many third dates, which is the threshold, according to what I've heard, for connecting in a—" He looked at the mayor, who was taking in this conversation with more than a little interest. "More physical way."

"So you're saying you didn't 'connect' with Kiki? Hard to believe since you had her room number at the lodge." Hey, he opened that door by stretching the boundaries of discretion.

"A gentleman always respects a lady's privacy. Especially about connecting—"

"Look, I'm not Phoebe," Mayor Loretta said. "I've heard the word *sex*. In fact, believe it or not, I've actually experienced it a time or two."

"Right. Because you're married." Faith's cheeks were burning with embarrassment. "Here's the thing—Phoebe is young and impressionable. Witnessing a parade of women going in and out of Sam's house would raise a lot of questions that I'm not prepared to answer right now."

"I think I can survive without female companionship while the evacuation order is in effect. We're only talking a day or two. Right?"

The mayor nodded. "That's the best guess right now. But fire is unpredictable."

"I'm grateful for the offer, Sam. Really. But it would probably be best if we stay with Loretta and Tom."

"Even though I have multiple bedrooms with actual beds? Not air mattresses on the floor."

The mayor looked puzzled. "Of course you're welcome, Faith, but it sounds as if you'd be more comfortable at Sam's until the danger is over."

Faith was comfortable teasing and tormenting him when he bought flowers from her. Being in his house didn't sound comfortable at all. "Phoebe has to be my first priority so—"

"Look, Faith, your aunt Cathy was my best friend," Loretta said. "When she was losing her cancer battle she made me promise to watch over you and Phoebe for her. And I swore I would make sure you were being taken care of. In this situation I have to say the best place for you is with Sam."

"Selfishly," he said, "you'd be doing me a favor."

"Really?" She didn't actually buy into that and was humoring him.

"I'm new in town and trying to fit in. Folks here take care of their own. It's a hallmark of Blackwater Lake. So let me be neighborly in order to win them over."

"He's got a point," the mayor agreed.

"And it's not an inconvenience." Sam gave her a look that probably melted female resistance like a Popsicle in the summer sun. "I'm sure the firefighters will get things under control pretty fast."

"And I really need to get an update on their progress." Loretta looked at her watch.

Faith felt ganged up on and wanted to dig in but there was no mistaking the worry and weariness in the other woman's face. She wouldn't add to it. "All right. If you think it's best, Loretta. Sam can earn points for being a good citizen."

"Good. That's settled." Loretta looked relieved. "I have to run."

Faith deliberately watched the mayor hurry to the lobby's double glass doors and quickly leave the building. She would have watched anything to put off having to face being alone with Sam Hart. It shouldn't feel different from all the other times she'd talked to him, but it did. Because she was going to move in with him.

Would Kiki be jealous? It was easier to think about

that than the nerves she was currently rocking. Activity was the best defense so she went back to shutting down the flower cart.

"Okay, then," she said. "I'm going to load up the van and take all this stuff back to my shop. Then I'll pick up Phoebe from summer camp."

"Do you want me to pick her up? Save time?" Sam asked.

"She's going to be scared so it would be best if I do it. Besides, you're a stranger and not on the list of people authorized to get her. She doesn't know you and that could cause more anxiety."

"Of course." He nodded and took a business card from his wallet. After writing something on the back he handed it over. "This is my address. I'll follow you to the shop and help unload the van."

"But—"

He held up a finger to stop her words. "I'm not sure what your deal is—whether you don't want help or just not from me. But this is about being neighborly so don't compromise my image."

"Okay. When you put it like that..."

After locking down the cart, Faith wheeled the flowers to her van parked in the lot behind the Hart financial building. She opened the vehicle's sliding door and stepped inside, then let Sam hand the vases and flowers in so she could secure them.

With his hands on the portable cart, he said, "I'll put this back inside, then meet you at the shop."

Part of her wanted to be snarky about him taking charge. The other part was glad he did. Because she probably wasn't thinking all that clearly, what with her house in danger of going up in flames.

So all she said was "Thanks."

Faith drove to downtown Blackwater Lake as fast as the

speed limit allowed and pulled the van into the parking area behind her primary shop on Main Street. She hopped out of the driver's side and by the time the rear door of Every Bloomin' Thing was propped open, Sam had driven into the lot and was getting out of his pricey luxury SUV. That was fast. Had he observed the speed limit?

At this moment she was too happy help had arrived to care. It meant she could get to her daughter faster. She reached into the van and started to grab a vase of flowers.

"Let me unload and you can put everything away. Since you know where it all goes that will probably be faster," he said.

He was right and she nodded. A short time later everything was secured inside. They walked out the back door of the shop then she turned the key in the deadbolt to lock it up.

"I'm going to get Phoebe now," she told him.

"Do you want me to go with you?"

"No."

The negative was automatic. If Loretta or almost anyone else in town had offered she would have accepted the moral support without question. But today she was afraid. Her home was in danger. That was bad enough, but she'd flirted with a different kind of danger when she'd flirted with Sam. It never occurred to her that she would ever be living with him, even for a short time. Damage control started right now.

"You've already done enough, Sam. Besides, I need to talk to her alone, prepare her before she meets you."

"Why? Do you think I scare small children?" He put his hands on his hips. "I have a niece who's not quite three and she isn't afraid of me."

"It's not that. I don't think it's a good idea to hit her with too much all at once." She shrugged. "Bad enough I have to break the news that her house could go up in flames, but then she meets a strange man and is going to stay in his house…"

His gaze narrowed. "Are you talking about Phoebe being nervous? Or you?"

"I'm an adult. I understand what's happening. She's just a kid and I want to reassure her that everything's all right."

"You know best," he said. "And you've got my card and cell number. Call if you need anything at all."

"Thanks."

Faith put a foot on the van's running board and slid inside, then closed the door. She turned her key in the ignition and drove slowly away, glancing quickly in her rearview mirror. Sam was standing there, almost protectively, watching her leave. Her heart did that fluttering thing, which didn't make her feel any better about accepting his offer of shelter.

Evacuating to the mayor's house or with old Brewster Smith and his wife, Aggie, would feel comfortable and normal. But Sam Hart was a bachelor. Even worse, she was attracted to him.

Sam had been watching out the front window for Faith so he opened the door before she could ring the doorbell. The little girl standing on the front porch beside her had to be Phoebe. Her Mini-Me had the same blond hair and freckles on her nose.

"Hi," he said to both of them, then smiled down at the little girl. "You must be Phoebe."

Long straight bangs caught in the thick eyelashes framing big, brown eyes that were wide with apprehension. "How did you know?"

"Your mother told me about you." Poor kid. No matter how the truth had been censored, she had to know that her home was in danger. That was scary for an adult let alone a child. "Come on in."

Sam pulled the door open wider and stepped back to let them pass. The little girl clutched her mother's hand tightly as she looked around wide-eyed.

"Wow. This is big." She was looking up at the chandelier in the two-story entryway. For the moment, awe distracted her from fear and worry.

He could keep the distraction going for a while because this *was* a big house. Glancing at Faith, he saw that she looked the tiniest bit impressed, too, and that didn't bother him a bit. "Would you like to see the rest of the place?"

Faith looked at her daughter who nodded eagerly. "Okay."

"Follow me." Sam noticed she was carrying a couple of bulging bags.

"Since we couldn't go home, I had to pick up some clothes and toiletries for us," Faith explained.

He held out his hand. "Let me take those for you."

"That's okay. I've got it."

"I can see that. But guys are supposed to carry things for girls."

"Why?" Phoebe asked. "Is that a rule?"

"No. But boys are usually bigger and stronger and it's the gentlemanly thing to do."

"Oh." The little girl thought about that and frowned. "At summer camp the girls carry stuff and the boys let us."

"Girls have to be able to take care of themselves," Faith explained. "It's called being self-reliant."

"And that's a good thing," Sam allowed. "But in certain situations, like now for instance, what with you being guests in my home, it's appropriate for a man to help a lady."

"And sometimes a lady just wants to tell a man to take a flying leap because she's perfectly capable of carrying her own things."

"Can I look at your house?" Phoebe was staring up at

them, clearly impatient and not the least bit interested in the undercurrents of the adult standoff.

"We can," he said. "Follow me."

"You can carry this if you want." Phoebe held out a pink backpack with two female cartoon characters on it, one in a sparkly turquoise dress.

"It would be my pleasure," he said, taking it from her. "This way."

He led them straight ahead to the kitchen and family room, with its leather corner group and two-story river rock fireplace.

"That's the biggest TV I ever saw," Phoebe said.

Sam looked down at her and realized that when you were small, everything must look gigantic. "I'll show you how to turn it on later."

Faith cleared her throat loudly and, when she had his attention, shook her head. "Sensitive electronic remote controls and an eight-year-old are not a good combination."

"She thinks I'm still a baby." The little girl made a face. "I'm not."

"I can see that. Maybe your mom would be okay with it if there's an orientation."

Phoebe frowned. "What's that?"

"I'll show you how to use it and you can practice for a while with me supervising. Your mom might be okay with that."

"I don't think so. Mom doesn't let me do very much. She's a little overprotective."

"Hey," Faith said. "I'm standing right here. And I'm not overprotective. Where did you hear that?"

"I don't know. Around. And anyway, in the car you told me not to touch anything in his house," the child said. "And that's kind of hard unless I stand in the corner."

Sam looked from one to the other and said, "I've never been the rose between two thorns."

"How long have you been waiting to drop that into a conversation with me?" One corner of Faith's beautiful mouth quirked up.

"I thought you'd like that one, plant lady. And, moving on—"

He showed them the rest of the downstairs, with its spacious home office and media room. On the second floor he took them past the master where he slept to the wing with three other bedrooms and a large open space set up as another entertainment area.

"How big is this house?" Faith asked.

"A little over five thousand square feet."

"No one else lives here with you?" Phoebe asked, wonder in her voice.

"You do now." He looked at her mom. "Told you I had lots of space. Do you want to pick out a room?"

"Yes!" Phoebe raced down the hall and disappeared around a corner.

Faith went after her and Sam realized he'd never had the opportunity to look at her from the back. She was always facing him with a counter in between them. She had quite a superior rear view and now he knew what he'd been missing all this time.

He caught up with them in the room that overlooked the front lawn with a spectacular view of Blackwater Lake beyond it. There was a queen-size bed, walk-in closet and bathroom.

"There's a bed in here even though no one lives here?" Phoebe asked.

"Yes." He'd never thought about that. Furnishing the whole house seemed like a good idea when you didn't want it to be a big, empty shell.

"I think you and I can share this room, Phoebs," her mother said.

"But no one is using that other room. The green one. Sam said so."

"I know, sweetie. But I know you. It seems like a good idea right now but when the sun goes down you're not going to want to be in there by yourself."

"I promise I will," Phoebe begged.

"I have an idea." Sam looked at Faith. "Not taking sides here, but how about if she tries sleeping in the green room. If you change your mind, you can always crawl in with your mom."

"You're okay with that?" Faith asked.

"Of course. There are five bedrooms in this house. I have one. The other four are up for grabs."

Faith was wearing an uncertain expression as she nodded. "I promise when we're able to go home, we'll leave the rooms in the same condition we found them."

"Don't sweat it. I have a cleaning service." He set the pink backpack just inside the door of the green room.

"Okay." She smiled. "I'm grateful for your hospitality."

"Don't do that," he said.

"What? Thank you? It's the polite thing to do."

"Mommy always tells me to say thank you," Phoebe chimed in, then disappeared.

"I meant don't be nice to me," he told Faith. "It's just weird."

She laughed and for a few moments the tension in her expression disappeared. "Okay. I'll see what I can do."

"Mommy! There's a pool!"

"Phoebe?" She set her bags inside the doorway then called out, "Where are you?"

"In the big family room upstairs." The reply was muffled because she was around a corner and down the hall.

Sam put his palm to the small of Faith's back as they walked in the direction the little girl had gone. Touching her wasn't the dumbest thing he'd ever done, but it ranked fairly high up on the list. Awareness tingled in his fingers and crackled through his entire body. The whole point of opening his home to evacuees was to be neighborly. But touching her opened up something else, too. What had she called it? Oh, yes. Connecting in a physical way. The idea of that was entirely too appealing.

They found the little girl looking out the window at the backyard. The pool *was* big, one could say proportional to the rest of the property. He'd put it in for swimming laps and staying in shape. Also for summer parties and entertaining. And he was particularly proud of the built-in barbecue area and outdoor kitchen. There was also a covered patio and the yard was meticulously landscaped.

"Do you want to go outside?" Sam asked.

"Yes!" Phoebe didn't wait for further invitation. She took off ahead of them.

"Does she always speak in exclamation points?" he asked.

"Only when she gets her choice of bedroom and there's a pool outside."

Shoulder to shoulder, he and Faith followed, but this time Sam made it a point not to touch her. No one could say he didn't learn from his mistakes.

They met Phoebe at the family room's French doors, where she waited impatiently for him to unlock and open them. Outside, he watched the little girl stop and stare, taking everything in. It wasn't long before she moved closer to the water.

"Don't fall in," Faith warned.

Sam positioned himself close enough to pluck her out if necessary. "I have arm floaties for my niece if you want them."

"I can swim," Phoebe informed him. "My camp is at the lake and they taught me how."

"Good."

"Can I go swimming?" she asked.

"That's up to your mom."

"As long as there's an adult outside with you." Faith held up a hand, obviously aware protest was coming. "I know you're not a baby and can swim but water safety starts with never swimming alone."

"Your mom is right," Sam agreed.

"Okay. They told us that at camp, too." The little girl moved closer to him and looked up. "I like you, Sam."

"You're not so bad yourself, Squirt."

"None of my friends have a pool," she continued.

"What am I? Chopped liver? I thought I was your friend," he protested.

"You are. So," she continued, "does that mean I can go swimming anytime I want? As long as there's an adult there with me?"

"Whoa, kiddo," Faith said. "Remember we're only here temporarily. One day. Maybe two. Just until the fire is contained and it's safe to go home."

"You told me that a million times, Mom." She went over to explore the outdoor kitchen.

"You know, Faith, she's welcome to come swimming anytime," Sam offered.

Faith glanced at her daughter, who was opening drawers and the outdoor refrigerator and too far away to hear. "Please don't make promises to my child that you don't intend to keep."

"I have every intention of keeping that promise."

"Maybe right this minute," she said. "But life will go back to normal and there will be female visitors. Two strikes and out. Breakup bouquets and peonies. A promise to a little girl could get in the way of that lifestyle and your women."

"So much for you being nice to me."

"I wasn't being mean. Just stating a fact." She looked

past him and frowned. "Phoebe Catherine, I told you not to touch anything. Stop right now."

Sam watched her walk away and realized several things, starting with the fact that Phoebe's father didn't seem to be in the picture. One could presume that Faith had been let down big-time by a man. The self-reliant message was a big clue, as was the warning to keep his promise to her child or she'd come after him like a pack of wolves. She hadn't actually said that but the expression in her eyes had conveyed the message loud and clear.

But she needed to realize a few things, too. There weren't as many women in his life as she thought and he made sure none of them had expectations. He wasn't a bad guy and wanted Faith to know it. He was very careful not to make promises he couldn't keep. Starting with commitment.

Very soon he was going to set her straight about all of the above.

Chapter Three

Faith left work early the next day and headed to the fire staging area for a volunteer shift. At the base of the mountain she saw auxiliary fire trucks parked, and soot-covered, exhausted men slumped against them. Not far away there was a tarp, and underneath it were picnic benches and a propane steam table where food was being kept warm. After parking her van she got out and instantly was hit by a gust of hot wind that whipped her hair around. She slid a scrunchie from the pocket of her jeans and pulled the strands off her face into a ponytail, then walked over to the food area.

Delanie Carlson, who owned the local pub, Bar None, transferred a case of water bottles to a large insulated chest then poured a bag of ice in to cool them down quickly. At a stove stirring food she saw Lucy Bishop, chef and co-owner of the Harvest Café. Both women were good friends.

"It's really windy." That was stating the obvious and there was no point in doing that. They all knew what could happen and worry clawed at her. But she was here to do her part and take her mind off the fact that she could lose her home.

"What can I do?" she asked Lucy.

"Organize the paper plates and utensils for an assembly line. The firefighters are on a regular rotating schedule," the blue-eyed blonde said. "They need the breaks to cool off, eat and rest. Otherwise someone could make a deadly mistake."

"That sounds like Desmond Parker's doing. Everyone says he's a really good fire captain," Faith said.

"That's the rumor. I've seen for myself that he's hardcore about enforcing breaks." Lucy's tone said she respected him for doing a great job, but in other areas he was not deserving of her high opinion.

"Ice is really cold." Delanie joined them, shaking water off her hands.

"That's kind of the point." Faith smiled.

The auburn-haired woman returned it. "But I wish someone could invent ice that didn't give you frostbite."

"Get ready, ladies. We're almost up." Lucy pointed to a group of men who had just disembarked from a truck that'd pulled into the staging area. They were wearing thick coats and pants plus heavy boots and other firefighting gear. Their first stop was a comfort station, where they poured water over their heads. Then the grimy jackets were shucked before they lined up at the food station.

Faith handed the first guy a plate and plastic utensils wrapped in a paper napkin. "How are you?"

"Hot. Hungry. Beat."

There was nothing else to say. Clearly he didn't have the energy to make small talk. She couldn't imagine how difficult the working conditions were.

Lucy piled the man's plate with food. It wasn't fancy but there was plenty. "Is there progress?"

"Hard to tell."

"There's a table over there with cookies," Delanie said, handing him an icy-cold water bottle. "And thanks for what you're doing."

"It's my job," he said simply.

"I know. But thanks. When this is over there's a round of drinks waiting for you guys at Bar None."

"Then we better get it over." His smile was weary.

For the next hour they served food, distributed water, accepted and organized food donations dropped off by concerned townspeople—and tried to lighten the load of every exhausted man and woman who was taking a break from the fight to save other people's homes and property from the fire.

Faith handed Desmond Parker a plate. He was the last man in this group, having waited until each of his guys had been taken care of. "Hi, Des."

"Hey, Faith."

"You look terrible." Her heart went out to him, but she hadn't meant to be so blunt. "I mean that in the nicest possible way. No offense."

He laughed. "None taken. I get it."

The man was in his thirties and had dark hair and blue eyes. Suspenders from his insulated pants seemed to highlight his broad shoulders, and his black T-shirt with BLFD—Blackwater Lake Fire Department—in bold white letters stretched tightly across his impressive chest. He was really handsome, even with the grime all over him. But Faith didn't feel a single flutter in the vicinity of her heart. Not like she did with Sam.

"How's it going?" she asked him.

"This is a tough one." Worry etched in the soot on his face told her it was worse than he would say. "Wind speeds pick up late in the afternoon and the fire jumps from hill to hill. That stretches our resources even thinner."

"So no containment yet."

"Maybe ten percent." His eyes darkened. "Don't you live somewhere near Crawford's Crest?"

"Yeah. Phoebe and I had to evacuate yesterday." A vision of Sam Hart pouring her coffee that morning flashed before her eyes. He was a very good host, but with all the women in his life he'd probably had a lot of practice. "Do you have any information about the area?"

"Sorry." He shook his head. "Got my hands full on the fire line."

"My bad. I shouldn't have asked."

"Don't worry about it. Of course you want news about your property. Wish I had something for you." His expression was sympathetic. "Well, I better get some food."

"Right. Sorry. Didn't mean to hold you up."

Faith watched Lucy fill his plate without saying a word to him. That was weird since she'd chatted with the other guys who came through—teased and talked and lifted their spirits. But not a syllable or a smile for Des Parker. What was up with that?

When the rush was over the three of them replenished supplies at their respective stations, then looked at each other.

Delanie glanced at the plume of red-tinged smoke that just seemed to expand and obscure any blue in the sky. "I wish there was more I could do to help."

"You've already taken people into your home," Lucy pointed out.

"So have you."

"The families you gave shelter to are pretty lucky," Faith pointed out. "There are worse places to stay than with the proprietors of Bar None and the Harvest Café."

"Yup." Delanie nodded. "Except for the part where they could lose their homes and all their worldly possessions."

"Oh my God, Faithie." Lucy pressed a hand to her forehead. "I forgot. Your house is in the evacuation zone, isn't it?"

"Yes." She kept trying to tell herself that as long as she and Phoebe were healthy and safe nothing else mattered, that worry wouldn't do any good. But sometimes it slipped past her defenses.

"How are you?" Delanie's voice was full of concern. "Where did you and Phoebe go? You should have called me."

"Or me," Lucy said.

"The mayor came to tell me personally and as it happened Sam Hart was there. Loretta had something to do with him opening his home to us." He'd actually been very gracious about the whole thing and she wasn't sure why that was so surprising.

"I've seen him in Bar None."

"And the café." There was a "hmm" in Lucy's voice. "He doesn't seem the sort to be pushed around. Not even by Madam Mayor."

Delanie nodded her agreement. "I know what you mean. The man owns a successful financial company with a lot of employees. It's highly unlikely she could intimidate him into something he didn't want to do."

"You're both right. And obviously observant," Faith said. "I didn't mean to imply that the mayor shamed him into volunteering. Like I said, she came by my cart in the lobby of Sam's building to tell me I couldn't go home. She said she had a full house but could find floor space and air mattresses for Phoebe and me."

"So he *was* shamed," Lucy said.

"Maybe. I don't know. He spontaneously offered because he has a big house. And Loretta said it would be a relief not to have to worry about us, what with all the problems she was handling." Then Sam had made his case to talk her into staying with him.

"So you were there last night," Delanie commented. "How was it?"

"He didn't lie about it being big. And beautiful." And the man had gone out of his way to make sure they were comfortable and had everything they needed. He'd even cooked dinner.

"What's he like?" Lucy asked, as if reading her mind. "I mean, obviously he's nice looking."

"Nice?" Delanie shook her head. "You can do better than that, Luce."

"You're absolutely right." The blonde looked appropriately chastised. "This whole fire crisis has thrown me off my game. Sam Hart is so hot he could melt a lesser woman than me into a pathetic puddle at his feet."

Faith would admit, if only to herself, that she'd dipped a toe into that puddle. "And what's your point?"

"We want details. What is it like living with him?" Delanie folded her arms over her chest. "Did you see him naked this morning?"

"Of course not." But wouldn't that have been something. "And I'd hardly call it living together—"

"Don't split hairs. You both spent the night under the same roof. By any definition that is living together."

"Temporarily. That's quite a different dynamic."

"Don't rain on our parade," Lucy begged. "We're doing our best to live vicariously. And if there's a little matchmaking behind it, where's the harm? The least you can do is meet us halfway."

"This is where I tell you guys to get a life."

Delanie grinned. "I have all the life I want, thanks. And right now yours has gotten exciting. In an interesting way, not the part where your house is in danger. And, for the record, we're trying to take your mind off that. So, when life gives you lemons…"

"What she's trying to say," Lucy interrupted, "is that details would be most appreciated."

"I love you guys for trying to take my mind off things, but I still don't know what you want me to say." Faith looked from one woman to the other. "Is he handsome? Check. Does he have money? Judging by his house that gets a big check mark, too."

"How's Phoebe doing with it?" Lucy asked.

"Pretty well, all things considered. She's distracted by the house and pool. He even let her use the TV remote." She couldn't help smiling at the memory of him explaining what each button meant and letting her daughter push them, even though that meant jumping through hoops to restore settings. "She's Team Sam."

"He sounds like a good guy," Lucy summed up and Delanie nodded her agreement.

Faith gave them a warning look. "He and I are just friends. I've gotten to know him because he buys a lot of flowers for women."

"Sounds romantic to me." Lucy stirred the beans on the steam table.

"Trust me. It's not. Just a gimmick. A smoke screen. An elaborate ruse in which he appears to participate but really doesn't at all."

"How do you know?"

"He told me. I asked him, as a flower professional, whether or not I should look forward to the revenue a wedding could generate."

"You didn't." Delanie's expression oozed admiration. "Look at you going all TMZ on him."

"What did he say?" The other woman stopped stirring. Apparently that revelation had the persnickety chef's rapt attention.

"It was a definite *no* on walking down the aisle."

"Oh, pooh. That's not what I wanted to hear. So I

shouldn't count on a wedding reception catering contract from him."

"Sad but true, ladies. Commitment is not on his to-do list."

Her friends looked disappointed, but Faith was fine with it. Better than fine, actually. This conversation had put things into perspective. The fact that neither she nor Sam was open to romance was tremendously freeing. She could be herself around him because there was no chance of any weird man/woman stuff.

Sam was trying to decide whether or not to worry.

At breakfast Faith had told him she was going to volunteer at the fire staging area after work, do what she could for the firefighters. Her lobby cart had been locked up several hours ago when he'd left work for the day.

Was it time to do something stupid and go look for her?

Before he could make up his mind, he heard the front door open and female voices in the entry. He'd given her a key and moments later Faith and Phoebe joined him in the kitchen.

"Hi, Sam." Phoebe gave him a wave.

"Hey, Squirt." He looked at Faith. "Long day?"

"Yeah." She looked tired, dirty and worried.

Again, Sam had the most absurd urge to pull her into his arms and tell her that everything would be all right. "Any news on your house?"

"No. And the evacuation order is still in effect." She shrugged. "The guys have been too busy saving houses to keep track of the ones lost."

Were the black streaks on her cheeks and chin soot? He frowned. "How close were you to the fire?"

"A couple of miles, I think. Why?"

"Because you smell like smoke."

"You should have been in the car." Phoebe wrinkled her cute freckled nose. "Stinks in there now."

Humor relaxed the tension on Faith's features. "You do realize that I was doing a good thing? Serving food to firefighters who are working very hard to save our home. And your toys."

"Uh-huh." Phoebe looked unrepentant. "You still smell like smoke."

"The wind is brutal."

Sam thought about that. "If it was blowing smoke in your direction, doesn't that mean the fire was headed toward where you were?"

"Are you asking whether it was safe?"

"Was it?"

"Of course."

He hadn't given in to stupid and gone to look for her, but now it was coming out of his mouth, this unreasonable concern for her safety. He was going to stop now. "Okay."

"The problem is the wind keeps changing direction. It's one of the reasons they're having such a hard time getting a handle on containment."

"I see."

"Until the crisis is over, there's a volunteer schedule," Faith said.

"So you'll be going back into the fire area?" He glanced at Phoebe, keeping his voice conversational so as not to alarm her. But for reasons he didn't want to examine too closely, he needed reassurance. And yes, he was aware that the stupid was continuing in spite of his effort to suppress it.

"Everyone is pitching in." She shrugged as if that explained everything.

"Can't you just make a casserole? Or cookies?"

She glanced at her daughter now. Phoebe was staring up wide-eyed. "The firefighters have safety protocols in place. That's one of the few things they can control. It's the variables like wind and thick, dry underbrush that are giving them fits."

"Mommy, you don't get too close, do you?"

"No, absolutely not." She thought for a moment. "Do you remember Des Parker?"

Phoebe's forehead furrowed in thought. "Is he the rancher who took you to the Grizzly Bear Diner?"

"No. That was Logan Hunt."

"He's my cousin," Sam volunteered. Estranged, but still family. Although that distinction didn't ease the feeling of disapproval sliding through him.

"Really?" Faith's eyes widened. "I didn't know that."

"Long story," he said. "So who's Des Parker?"

"The fire captain."

"I remember," Phoebe said. "He let me sit in the fire truck on the Fourth of July and bought us ice cream. And Valerie Harris babysat me and you went out to dinner with him."

"Yes."

"I like him," her daughter said.

Funny, Sam thought, he didn't. "So he's not going to let anything happen to his girlfriend."

"It's not like that. And in case you're wondering, there was no breakup bouquet. Come to think of it, that would be awkward. Making it for myself." Faith laughed. "No, my point is that he's cautious and wouldn't let anything happen to anyone on his watch."

Sam didn't miss the look she gave him that said he was being weird, but he already knew.

Phoebe wrinkled her nose again, apparently satisfied that her mother was in good hands. "You still stink."

"It's not that bad." She looked at Sam.

"I wasn't going to say anything…" He rested his hands on the granite-topped island between them. "However, I strongly suggest you soak in a hot bath while Phoebe and I cook dinner."

"You cook? I thought last night was a fluke."

"No." Sam took a little satisfaction from her obvious surprise. "I'm a bachelor."

"And yet I, the plant lady, know that—" she glanced at her child, obviously trying to figure out how to give her comment a G-rated delivery "—from time to time you have visitors who *can* cook."

"That is blatant gender profiling." He smiled at her unease. "Some of the world's best chefs are men. And I actually like to cook."

"I can help, Mommy. Please let me do it." The eight-year-old was quivering with excitement. "And Sam is right. You need a bath."

"And the child becomes the parent." Faith tenderly traced a finger down her daughter's cheek. "Two against one. Fortunately for both of you I'm in the mood to get rid of this grime. I won't be long."

Sam watched until her slender shoulders and excellent backside disappeared from sight. She was a smart, beautiful woman raising a child on her own. As far as he could tell there was no father in the picture. Why? For that matter, it was clear from what Phoebe had said that she dated. His cousin had inherited the Hart good looks and his mother's integrity. His father, Sam's uncle, had the morals of an alley cat and Logan had distanced himself from the Harts a long time ago. He was a very successful rancher and from a woman's perspective would be a good catch.

Des Parker was a question mark because Sam had never met him. What was Faith's relationship with the two men? He really didn't like that he was acutely curious, which was only a small step up from jealousy.

"Sam?" A small, firm voice interrupted his thoughts. "Are you listening?"

He looked at the little girl. "Yes."

"I want to help. But Mommy won't let me touch sharp stuff."

"That leaves out knives, then." He thought for a moment. "How about setting the table?"

"Okay."

Since plates and glasses were too high for her, he ended up getting everything down then backed off and let her put it all on the round oak table in the nook.

When she finished, she came to stand by the counter where he was working. "Whatcha doing?"

"I'm making fried chicken the easy way. After I dip the pieces in this stuff, it goes on a cookie sheet and into the oven."

"Are you making vegetables?" she asked suspiciously.

There was a loaded question. More data was required before answering. "Do you like them?"

"No."

"Hmm. Does your mom make you eat them?"

"Yes." It didn't seem possible for such a small, sweet face to hold that much loathing and hostility.

"They have vitamins and minerals that make you strong and healthy."

"That's what my mom says. They still make me want to throw up."

"I feel your pain." He thought about what he'd planned for tonight. "What's your opinion of corn on the cob?"

"I like that. We have these things that go in the ends so you can hold it better. But they're in my house." Phoebe's anxiety that her house might be gone was easy to read in her expression.

Sam wanted to fix things so this little girl didn't have to worry about whether or not all of her worldly possessions were gone. But he wasn't God. All he could do was fix this moment for her.

"I have corn holders. In that drawer." He pointed out the one closest to the table. "Why don't you put them by the plates?"

She opened the drawer and spotted them. "They're sharp."

"Technically, but you're not going to cut anything with them. I think you're big enough to do the job without hurting yourself."

"Hurt yourself on what?" Faith walked into the kitchen. Her blond hair was a shade darker because it was still wet and the store tags were still hanging from her T-shirt and sweatpants.

The jeans he'd always seen her in were a good look but what she was wearing now hugged every curve in soft, clingy material. His fingers ached to find out for himself if she felt as good as he thought she would.

"Mommy." Phoebe proudly held up the sharp objects. "Sam has corn-on-the-cob holders. They're animals, see? It's a cow. This one is the head and here's the tail."

"Very cute." She met his gaze. "Something so whimsical seems out of character for a high-powered businessman like you."

"I've got layers," he said.

"Apparently." She looked at Phoebe. "You're not supposed to touch anything sharp and pointy."

"Sam said I could. And I didn't hurt myself." She held up her boo-boo-free hands. "See?"

"I did give her permission," Sam said. "It was actually the lesser of two evils. I wanted to give her a moratorium from vegetables while she's here."

"I see what you mean." She smiled at her daughter. "Good job, Phoebs."

"Can I watch TV now?"

Sam put the chicken in the oven. "Dinner won't be ready for about forty minutes."

"Okay, then, kiddo."

"Yay!" She ran into the family room and carefully picked up the remote, handling it as he'd shown her.

When they were alone, Sam said, "Speaking of sharp things, you could use scissors."

Faith looked down at her hastily purchased clothes. "I forgot to pull them off."

He grabbed a pair from a drawer and moved close. "Let me."

The sweet scent of her freshly washed hair filled his head and twisted his senses into knots. Without thinking it through, he grabbed the tag that was just inside the neckline of the shirt to cut it off and his fingers brushed her skin. Her eyes darkened and her lips parted slightly. He was almost sure her breath caught for a moment. He knew for a fact that his did.

She swallowed once and glanced at the tag on the waist of her pants. "I'll get that one."

"Okay."

She took the scissors, careful not to touch him, and quickly did the job. It was time for him to break the spell so he opened a bottle of red wine, letting it breathe normally, which was more than he could say for himself. Then he took three glasses from a cupboard, one of them a champagne flute, and poured clear soda into it.

"For Phoebe," he explained. "Just this once. Because she's evacuated."

Before Faith could say no, he brought it to the little girl on the leather sofa in the family room. "Tonight is a special occasion."

"What?" She took the glass he held out.

"I get to have the pleasure of your company for dinner."

"Wow." Carefully she took a sip. "I promise I won't spill."

"I know you won't."

He walked back into the kitchen where Faith stood with her back braced against the island. She was giving him a look. "What?"

"You're very good at this," she said.

The tone didn't make her words sound like a compliment so he decided to clarify his actions in a positive way. "If you mean taking care of friends going through a rough time, then yes I am."

"I actually meant you're quite practiced at charming women."

There was a whole lot of subtext in those words. "Charm isn't a bad thing."

"It is if it's not sincere." She folded her arms over her chest.

"Look, as far as I'm concerned we've become friends. So if what you see in my behavior is charm in a bad way, then I'm not sure what I can do about that."

"Just stop it."

"I can't be what I'm not," he pointed out.

"Neither can I."

"Okay." Sam dragged his fingers through his hair. He was going to say this and let the chips fall wherever. "You don't have to tell me I'm right, but I think there's a better-than-even chance some guy did you wrong."

"You don't—"

He held up a hand to stop her. "You're right. I don't know for sure. But the fact that defensiveness is your default position makes it a very good possibility."

She didn't respond to that.

"I assure you that I have no ulterior motives. I value your friendship and don't want things to get awkward between us. There's nothing to worry about from me and you can take that promise to the bank." He smiled. "No pun intended."

Her lips curved up slightly. "Okay."

Sam's word was important to him and he didn't give it lightly. He'd drawn a line in the sand and wouldn't cross it, even though the idea of kissing her had occurred to him. But he was sure there was a jerk in her past and he wouldn't be another one who played her.

When she could go back to her house in a day or two, this feeling would pass. There was no doubt in his mind that he could resist her for that short a time.

Chapter Four

"You didn't have to come with me and volunteer to help feed the firefighters." Faith glanced at Sam in the driver's seat, which was appropriate since this was his car. Although she was pretty sure that's where he sat in every part of his life.

"This is my town now and I want to pitch in." He slid her a look but the expression in his eyes was hidden by the dark aviator sunglasses. Very sexy glasses that amped up his appeal by a lot. "I want to make sure the firefighters' staging area is a safe distance from the fire line."

"You don't trust Des Parker?"

"I don't know him." There was a hint of disapproval in his voice.

That was an interesting negative reaction to someone he'd never met. "He's a good guy."

"Jury's out on that. All I know is you were pretty smoky when you got home last night."

"That would sound so much better if you'd said I was smokin' hot."

Sam didn't look at her but the corners of his mouth curved up. "You'll do. And I'm here to make sure you're not literally smokin'."

He navigated the winding two-lane road in a confidently masculine way that made her stomach quiver in that feminine way it did when fascinated by a guy. Admittedly that reaction was just plain stupid, but, sadly, too real. The best thing she could say about the inconvenient feeling was that it took her mind off worrying about what condition her home was in.

But as they got closer to the staging area, visibility was reduced because of smoke hanging in the air and it got noticeably thicker every mile. The wind wasn't as bad, but it was still a factor in battling the blaze.

"I heard firefighters are coming from as far away as California and Oregon to help put this thing out." Sam glanced over.

"That's the rumor."

"They'll get it contained."

"Sure doesn't feel that way right now," she said.

"It won't burn forever."

"You can't know that."

"Wow." Sam glanced over again. "I didn't take you for a glass-half-empty kind of person."

"It's hard to be chipper and perky and optimistic when everything you have in the world might be gone."

"I know. But you have to stay strong."

"Says who?" She was feeling angry and resentful and looking to take it out on someone. It was his bad luck that he was in the line of fire, no pun intended. "Do you have any idea what it feels like to face the possibility of losing everything? Even with insurance there will be out-of-pocket expenses that I can't afford. You would only have to write a check. Chump change."

"I admit that having access to more resources makes the prospect less daunting."

Well, pickles. She'd expected him to be all sunshine and unicorns, not agree with her. Now what was she going to argue with him about?

"So, I met Kiki."

"Did you?" The corners of his mouth curved up.

"Yes. When I delivered the breakup bouquet."

"I see."

Faith wanted more of a reaction so she could push back on something because she was really in the mood to push back. "Don't you want to know what my impression of her was?"

He shrugged. "Since I won't be seeing her again, discussing it is like shutting the barn door after the horse got out."

"I can see why you'd think that, but you could look at it like a debrief. Analyze what went wrong in order to not make the same mistake."

He nodded slowly. "That logic would be sound if I considered her a mistake."

"And you don't?"

"Look at it this way." He thought for a moment. "When you buy a dress, you try it on. See if it fits and that you like how it feels. That's how I think of dating."

"Like trying on a pair of jeans?" She crossed her arms over her chest.

"Yes."

"So Kiki was nothing more than a fitting?"

"In a way." His tone was unrepentant.

"I found her to be very pretty and nice. It seems so wrong to categorize her like that."

"How else are you going to know what works?" he defended.

"Give someone a chance. Two dates is like making a decision on pants when you only try on one leg."

"Why risk trying on the other leg and becoming emotionally attached?"

"Oh. You're one of those," she said, nodding knowingly.

"What?" He glanced over, obviously fighting a grin. "You make me sound like a nonorganic vegetable at a health food convention."

Faith laughed, something that had seemed a long shot a few minutes ago. "I'll put a finer point on it. You're one of those men who is afraid of commitment."

"On the contrary. I'm not afraid, just choosing not to participate."

"That's just spin." Her words challenged even though she remembered his adamant admission that marriage wasn't for him. "You're afraid. Admit it."

"No." He made a left turn into an open area with heavy equipment, fire trucks and cars. "And we're here. Not a moment too soon."

Faith was jolted back to reality. Thanks to Sam, for a few minutes she'd managed to put aside the crisis hanging over her.

They exited his luxury SUV and headed for the volunteer area. She was put to work serving food again. Sam unloaded cases of bottled water from a truck and stacked them. Another truck arrived with ice and he unloaded bags, then filled insulated chests and tubs with it to cool down the water.

When Faith could sneak a glance at him she took full advantage. Watching Sam Hart work up a sweat was pure cotton candy for the eyes. And as distractions went, the sight of him was effective and exactly what a worried girl needed. She imagined he looked all CEO powerful behind his office desk in the building he owned. After today, she knew for a fact that he was pretty darn drool-worthy doing manual labor. And speaking of eye candy, a peek at him without a shirt might satisfy her sweet tooth.

When there was a break in the action, he grabbed two bottles of cold water and wandered over. He opened one and handed it to her.

"Thanks." She took a long drink then pressed her lips together, blotting the excess moisture. She noticed a muscle in his jaw jerk as he watched her and wondered about that but decided to ignore it. "I needed this. It's hot."

"There's an understatement." His voice was hoarse, probably from the smoky air. "And those guys fighting the fire have on all that heavy gear."

"I can't even imagine how they do it," she agreed. "So you think Des picked a safe place for the volunteers to be?"

"Yes." He shrugged. "It's a major fire and there's a lot of smoke. Phoebe is going to have a lot to say to both of us."

"She might not call you out. Right now you're her hero. Speaking of that—" Faith spotted a familiar firefighter walking toward them "—here comes one of our bravest now. Hi, Des."

"Hey, Faith."

Sam frowned at the man who stopped beside them. But he held out his hand. "We haven't met, but I've heard good things about you. I'm Sam Hart."

The other man took the offered hand. "Desmond Parker. Nice to meet you. I've heard about you, too. Welcome to Blackwater Lake. That new office building of yours is impressive."

"Can't complain. Pretty boring compared to what you do. You've got a tough gig right now, though. How's it going?"

"Frustrating." He took off his helmet and dragged his fingers through his sweaty, matted dark hair. "The wind is still making it a challenge to keep up with the fire. It keeps jumping around. The conditions are unpredictable." An expression slid into his eyes when his gaze met hers and it looked an awful lot like pity.

Faith had a feeling she wasn't going to like the answer but she had to ask. "Is there any news yet? About my neighborhood?"

"Yeah," Des said. "It's not good."

Her stomach dropped. "What?"

"The fire swept through Crawford's Crest. There are houses burned to the ground. Some have damage. I don't think any of them came through without a scratch. I don't have addresses because—" He looked down and shook his head. "There wasn't time to sort it out for folks."

"I know, Des. I—" Her voice caught.

"I'm so sorry." He squeezed her arm sympathetically. "I wish we could have pushed it back."

"You did everything you could."

"Maybe you're one of the lucky ones with minor damage," he said hopefully.

"Maybe."

But not likely, she thought. Sam was right. She was a glass-half-empty girl. It was better to accept the worst and be pleasantly surprised than to be shocked in a bad way.

"I have to go," he said. "Wish the news was better—"

"It's okay. Thanks for the update. And, please, take care of yourself. Be safe."

"Will do."

Fortunately there wasn't time to think about the worst because there was another group of dirty, tired, hungry men behind Des who'd just arrived from the front line. She got busy serving everyone and that took her mind off things. But a little while later she and Sam were relieved by other volunteers and walked back to his car.

She was fine until he opened the passenger door for her. The simple gesture would have been lovely under normal circumstances, but for some reason right now it highlighted that she was all alone. No one ever opened her door. She was the grown-up who handled things by herself. This life-changing emergency was no different. Tears filled her eyes and there was no way to hide them from Sam. She put her hands over her face.

"Faith—It's okay."

"It's n-not. You don't know that."

"But I know you and Phoebe are fine. The rest can be fixed."

"It doesn't feel that way right now." She dropped her hands and met his gaze, feeling the wetness rolling down her cheeks, probably making tracks through the grime. "The worst part is not knowing. Whether or not it's livable or we're homeless—" Her voice wavered, cutting off more words.

"Don't borrow trouble." In the next instant Sam reached out and pulled her close, wrapping his arms around her. "Everything will be all right. I know it's hard, but try not to worry."

He was strong and reassuring and she was probably going to regret liking it so darn much. But he was peace and serenity, heaven in a world gone to hell. One minute she'd felt completely alone and the next she was in his arms. Just this once she was going to appreciate being reassured by a man who was holding her.

Call her Scarlett O'Hara but tomorrow she'd worry about reinforcing her resistance to this man. It didn't seem all that important right now.

"How am I going to tell Phoebe?"

Sam looked down. "Can you wait until you know for sure what's going on?"

"She knows I came here to volunteer and will ask for news about our house. I can't lie. But how am I going to tell her this?"

* * *

After leaving the crisis command center Sam drove to Cabot Dixon's ranch, where Phoebe was going to summer camp. He was doing his best to act normal, to behave as if holding Faith in his arms had been nothing but brotherly. She was every guy's little sister, right?

That's not what his body was saying. Just before he'd held her, he'd told her not to borrow trouble. Feeling her soft curves pressed against him was like walking up to trouble and spitting in its eye. It wasn't the first time he'd had the urge to comfort her. When the mayor had given her the bad news about evacuating, he'd wanted to pull her close then but he'd managed to resist. What he'd done a few minutes ago proved that his self-control with Faith was deteriorating.

But as he drove beneath the sign that said "Dixon Ranch" and continued up the rolling hill to the compound of buildings, his thoughts turned to Phoebe. He admired Faith's instinct to be honest and knew that was the right thing to do. Still, Sam would have preferred to put off the conversation until it was clear what they were facing.

"You can park over there, by the house." Faith pointed to a hitching rail.

Just beyond it was a large two-story structure that had a wraparound porch with a white railing. There was a fan window above the front door. It was a nice place.

Sam turned off the car. "Do you want me to wait here?"

The expression in her eyes said she wanted to tell him she didn't need his support, or to depend on anyone for that matter. So it was a surprise when she said, "No. You can come."

They got out, walked up the steps and Faith knocked on the heavy oak door. It was answered moments later by a pretty woman with a baby in her arms.

"Hi, Faith." She had brown hair streaked with blond and

big green eyes. They darkened when she looked at him. "We haven't met. I'm Kate Dixon."

"Sam Hart. Nice to meet you." He smiled at the baby, a little girl judging by the pink dress and little pink bow in her blond hair. "Who's this?"

"Eve." She looked tenderly at the child, who had a finger in her mouth and was drooling. "She's nine months old and pretty much the star of the show around here. Her big brother, Tyler, dotes on her and she's daddy's little girl."

"I can see why." The only baby Sam had ever been around was his niece, Ellie's daughter, Leah. But this one was pretty cute, too, he noted.

"Speaking of the star..." Faith said. "Where's my little troublemaker?"

"Hi, Mommy. Hey, Sam." Phoebe appeared in the doorway and handed the baby a small pink doll. "I've been helping Kate with Eve."

"Have you? Good job." Faith smiled at her daughter but the strain was there if you knew to look.

"I'll go get my backpack." Phoebe disappeared inside.

"She's been a godsend," Kate said. "Cabot and Ty are hanging out with the summer campers who are boarding here. And Eve is really fussy. Teething, I think. Your daughter is so good and patient with her."

"I'm glad it helped to have her here. And I really appreciate you letting her stay longer so I could volunteer to help out the firefighters."

"We all do our part." Kate's expression oozed sympathy for what Faith was going through.

Sam was beginning to see that what the mayor had said about Blackwater Lake was true. People in this town pulled together when times were tough. If you couldn't go and help out in person, you took care of someone's child so they could go. He'd never experienced anything quite like this. Before moving here his idea of helping out was to write a check.

"Do you want to come in?" Kate offered. "I've got some iced tea or lemonade."

"No, thanks," Faith said. "I've imposed on you enough for one day."

"I'm sorry you didn't get a chance to meet my husband and son," she said to Sam.

"I'm sure I will soon."

It didn't escape his notice that Logan Hunt's spread wasn't far from here and he was pretty sure the two ranches shared a property line. After getting settled, one of his goals was to mend family fences with his cousin.

"I'm ready, Mommy." Phoebe had her pink backpack and stepped out onto the porch. "Are we going to Sam's house?"

Faith nodded. "It's still not safe for us to go home."

"Do you know anything about our house?" the little girl asked. "Is it okay?"

Faith hesitated, probably trying to find the right words. As quiet as she'd been on the way here, Sam was pretty sure she'd been searching for a way to tell the truth without traumatizing this child. In the end that wasn't possible.

"Phoebe, the news isn't good. The fire captain told me that they couldn't stop the flames and our neighborhood was affected."

"Is our house gone?" Her brown eyes filled with tears.

"Some houses are. He didn't know for sure about ours—" Faith stopped, no doubt trying to be strong in front of her child, but struggling to control her own emotions.

Sam had to do something to help her. He went down on one knee, to Phoebe's level. "The truth is, honey, that some of the houses just have damage, but are still there. The firefighters couldn't check because they're too busy trying to keep the fire from spreading to someone else's place—"

The little girl started to cry really hard, sobs that shook her little body. Sam didn't have to pull her in for a hug because she threw herself against him.

"I w-want to go home—"

"I know you do." Feeling helpless and out of his depth, he patted her back. Give him a spreadsheet or a boring business meeting any day. A little girl's tears and no way to fix them were a guy's worst nightmare. Just cut his heart out with a spoon. That would be a walk in the park compared to this. "It will be all right."

"No, it won't." She pulled away, tears rolling down her cheeks. "How can you say that?"

Sam was a numbers guy and they were specific. Maybe it would help to bring this conversation around to quantifiable terms and get her to open up at the same time. "Tell me what you think the worst would be."

"My things are burned up."

"Maybe not. We don't know for sure yet." He met her gaze. "But what things are you worried about specifically?"

She brushed at the tears on her face with the back of her hand as she thought about the question. "All my clothes. My *Frozen* pajamas."

"You keep your sleepwear in the freezer?" he asked, glancing at Faith, who smiled.

"No, silly," Phoebe said. "It's a movie. Anna and Elsa are on my nightgown." She thought some more. "All my playing dress-up stuff could be gone. My Ariel costume from last Halloween."

"Who's Ariel?" Three women, make that four if you counted the baby, looked at him as if he'd just crawled out from under a rock. He shrugged. "It's not in my frame of reference."

"She's a character from the animated movie *The Little Mermaid*," Kate told him.

"Ah. I'm going out on a limb and guessing that the costume didn't have shoes, so that's one less thing to worry about." He assessed Phoebe's expression and decided that attempt at humor had fallen flat. "What else?"

"Mommy bought me a new dress for the first day of school. It's pink."

"Of course it is," he said, looking at the color of her backpack. "Is that all?"

"No. My dollhouse came from Santa Claus. And there's a stroller for my babies. They're dolls but they look almost like a real baby. I have a cradle for them and a changing table. And—"

"Whoa." When the emotion level in her voice started to climb back into whimpering territory Sam was afraid quantifying might have backfired. Wow, there was a word he didn't want to say out loud. But it was time to change the direction of this conversation. "Honey, those are just things. They can be replaced."

"How?"

"From the store," he said patiently. "A marathon shopping trip will do the trick. The really important things are the ones you can't buy. You're okay. Your mom is okay. No one has been injured, not even the firefighters. That's a good thing because people can't be replaced."

"I guess," she said, humoring him.

"Bottom line—everyone who is important to you is fine."

"You're important to me, Sam."

The words went straight to his heart. Bam, the icy defensive wall shattered and instantly melted. "That means a lot to me, Squirt."

"And it's not just because I like your pool."

"Good to know." He glanced at the two women observing this little talk and saw approval in their eyes. It was a relief to know he was on the right track. "Have you ever heard the saying that every cloud has a silver lining? That means you can always find something positive in a bad situation. For you it's looking forward to an awesome shopping trip."

"Yeah." There was no conviction in the single word and her thin shoulders slumped.

"What else is on your mind?"

"What if my house is all burned up? What if I don't have anyplace to live? Or a bed?"

Sam glanced at Faith and the look on her face had him wanting to hold her again. He remembered her telling Phoebe that they would only have to stay with him until the fire was contained and it was safe to go home. No one had said anything about what would happen if there was no home to go back to. This little girl had gotten the meaning of the word *temporary* in relation to their current living arrangement. It was time to remove any uncertainty. He was now part of this town where pitching in was a hallmark of citizenship.

He met the little girl's worried gaze and willed her to know that he meant every word he was about to say. "There are things to be concerned about, but where you're going to live shouldn't be one of them, honey. You can live with me as long as you want."

Phoebe smiled and threw herself into his arms for a hug. "Thanks, Sam."

"You're welcome, Squirt." He couldn't imagine a business deal with a positive outcome that could make him feel any better than he did right at this moment. When she stepped back he said, "So, you're good?"

"Yes. I'm starving."

"Okay. Let's get you fed."

"Can I help make dinner again?"

"Sure." He watched her run down the steps to the car after saying goodbye to the baby.

"Wow." Kate's tone was full of admiration. "You have the father thing down pretty well."

"That was all luck." And yet he was feeling fairly proud of himself.

Until he looked at Faith. There was a frown on her face that put a big fat hole in his smug balloon.

Uh-oh.

Chapter Five

On the drive to Sam's house, Phoebe chattered away from the backseat. She loved the car with its cushy leather seats and rear air-conditioning that she could control by herself. Faith, on the other hand, was not jumping on the Sam-is-a-rock-star train. Where did he get off promising that they could stay with him as long as they wanted?

It sounded crazy to be annoyed at his generosity, which meant she could probably benefit from therapy. She was feeling just a tad shrewish when you factored in how incredibly sweet he'd been to Phoebe, reassuring her when Faith got so emotional.

The problem was he hadn't run it by her first. What if she wanted to make other arrangements? Part of her was relieved that they had somewhere to stay, even though leaving would be the smart move. Living with a man she was so attracted to was living on the edge. Love had never done her any favors and abstinence was her preferred form of protection.

She and Sam hadn't said anything to each other since leaving the Dixon Ranch but that was going to change when Phoebe was occupied and Faith could speak to him alone. However, finding time alone proved a challenge.

"Home sweet home." Sam pulled the SUV into the long curving driveway.

The beauty of the perfectly landscaped front yard made Faith wonder if a person could ever take this lush setting for granted. "You have a yard that is completely spectacular."

"Thank you." He hit a button located above the car's rearview mirror and the garage door lifted. After pulling in he said, "Who's hungry?"

"Did you forget?" Phoebe said. "I already said I'm starving."

"So you did. I am, too. What do you say to a backyard cookout and eating outside by the pool?"

"Cool. Can I have a hot dog?"

"Yes. Or a hamburger," he answered.

"What do you want, Mommy?"

So many things, Faith thought. Win the lottery. Give a piece of her mind to the mean girl in high school. World peace. And to not have these feelings for Sam. She glanced over at him and nearly sighed out loud at his lean, masculine profile. "I'd like to know how you can promise a cookout when there was no cookout food in the refrigerator this morning."

"I have an assistant." He pushed his aviator sunglasses to the top of his head.

"Her job is to go grocery shopping for you? That seems sexist."

"Faith." He sighed. "You have no faith. My assistant is named Jim and he volunteered to help so I could help. Everyone in town is pitching in."

And she wanted to bite her tongue. "That was very nice of him."

"Yes, it was." He opened the driver's-side door. "Let's go, ladies."

"I want to help." Phoebe had the volunteer spirit, but that might have more to do with a crush of her own on their host.

For the next half hour there was a flurry of activity and cooperation getting everything necessary on the patio table outside. Phoebe was in charge of paper plates, utensils and napkins. Faith made a green salad and cut up fruit. Sam assembled a platter of hot dogs, hamburgers and buns. There was no time to talk alone and Faith wouldn't be surprised if he'd taken that into consideration before announcing the menu. And there she was being skeptical again.

She was going to try to be positive, and it was positively a perfect evening. The air was cool and carried the scent of pine and wildflowers. In the distance there was a spectacular view of the Montana mountains. The sun had already set, but the yard was lined with lights and the patio cover had spotlights that pushed back the dark. From here the smoke wasn't visible and she did her best to put aside her fears about the fire. The glass of wine Sam gave her helped.

She couldn't resist teasing him. "Can we talk about your complete lack of information regarding current cultural references?"

"What information are we referring to?" Sam was sitting diagonally across the glass-topped patio table from her.

"Ariel? The costume didn't have shoes to worry about?"

"She's a mermaid, right?"

"Right." Phoebe pushed green salad around her plate without consuming a single leaf. Apparently a kid without toys could always find something to play with.

"So she doesn't need shoes." He shrugged. "Fins, not feet."

"Well, eventually she walks upright on two legs, but that's another conversation," Faith said. "And from *Frozen* you went to pajamas in the freezer?"

Phoebe giggled. "That was a good one, Sam."

"Thank you, Squirt." He smiled at her then looked at Faith. "I freely admit that animated movies are not something I know much about."

"Phoebe could give you a lot of information. She's seen them all." And had DVDs. Maybe.

"I bet she has." There was a longneck bottle of beer in front of him and Sam took a sip.

"My favorite is *Frozen*." The little girl yawned.

That's what Faith had been waiting for. "It's getting pretty close to bedtime, Phoebs. Time for your bath."

"But, Mommy—

"No argument. It's been a long day and you have camp tomorrow." And Faith needed to talk to Sam. "Do you remember how to fill the tub?"

"I'm not a baby."

"Okay. Take your plate inside then head upstairs. I'll be there after Sam and I clean everything up."

"Okay." The little girl did as requested, which meant she was too tired to protest.

When she'd disappeared inside, Sam said, "I'm going to take a wild guess that you and I cleaning everything up has nothing to do with dishes." Before she could confirm that, he added, "I meant what I said to her. You can stay here as long as you want."

"Sam, we talked about making promises to her," Faith reminded him.

"I meant it then and I still do. As long as you want," he repeated.

"What if I don't want to stay at all?"

"That's up to you."

"Right. My decision. But your unilateral announcement makes things harder."

"How?" He seemed sincerely confused.

"Look around." She indicated the lush yard trimmed with lights, the beautiful pool and waterfall. "Phoebe wouldn't want to leave this."

"That's the point. She doesn't have to."

"She does if I think that's best. Because you didn't run it by me first, making a move without her being upset becomes trickier."

"Do you want to go?"

Yes and no, she thought. No one in their right mind would want to leave this gorgeous, spacious luxury. But she was uneasy about staying. No matter how much square footage there was, she and Sam were both under the same roof.

"For now, no," she finally said. If she was being honest, his support earlier when breaking the news to the little girl about the fire had been a blessing. "Phoebe is settled in and feels secure. Rocking the boat when she's facing so much uncertainty doesn't seem like a good idea."

"I agree. And just so you know…" He leaned forward and rested his forearms on the table. "I enjoy having you here."

Something in his tone brushed over her nerve endings and sparked heat that burned through her. It was the husky edge to his voice that made her feel as if he might be attracted to her. An intensity in his eyes that hinted at more than simple friendship. Then there was that moment when he'd pulled her into his arms to comfort her. His strength made her feel safe and sheltered, something she couldn't ever remember experiencing before. It was too wonderful and too risky.

A one-sided crush was bad enough but something mutual was an invitation to give in to temptation. She needed to nip that in the bud.

"I bet you say that to all your women."

A wicked look stole into his eyes. "So, I met Des Parker."

"What's that supposed to mean?" The question was a stall. She knew exactly what he was doing. This was payback for her so-I-met-Kiki remark. It was unexpected and threw her off balance.

"It means that people who live in glass houses shouldn't throw stones."

"You're implying that I see a lot of men?"

"According to Phoebe. She mentioned Des and Logan Hunt." He held up two fingers as he counted them off. "Who knows how many more you're hiding."

"It's different," she defended.

"I don't see how."

"Don't forget that I've delivered your breakup bouquets. Trust me, it is different." Faith knew her rebuttal was sexist and a double standard. And she was on thin ice. She was sorry she'd brought it up. A change of subject seemed an excellent idea. If only she could think of something. "Just so we're clear, I'm not hiding anything. You're wrong about that."

"I don't think so. And now that you mention it, I'm noticing a pattern of behavior. Every time something comes up that you don't want to discuss, you bring up my dating habits." He finished off his beer, then set the empty bottle on the table and toyed with it. "It doesn't take a PhD in psychology to see that you have a story. A bad one. The only way your hiding would be more obvious is if you turned over furniture and ducked behind it."

Who knew a player like Sam could be so perceptive? That was unexpected. And she wasn't sure what to say. Faith stood and started consolidating their paper plates and set as much as possible on the large platter he'd used for the hot dogs and hamburgers. Her mind raced while her hands were busy.

He wasn't wrong and saying he was would be a lie. That's something she wouldn't do. Being on the receiving end of lies wasn't fun and she promised herself a long time ago not to do it.

"Look, Sam, before you go all Dr. Phil on me, I'll admit that I did have a bad experience with love." And she didn't just mean her ex-husband.

"Do you want to talk about it?"

"Only if you want to share why you're a confirmed bachelor."

He stood to help gather jars of condiments and plastic bags of buns. "Not particularly."

"Okay, then. Details aren't important. I just want you to know that I didn't mean to hurt your feelings. Don't take it personally."

"Deal."

His compliance took the wind out of her sails. Part of her had been tensed for a disagreement and she was a little annoyed that he'd removed any ammunition. Once again he was reasonable and rational, another positive trait to add to the list that included charming, sweet, sensitive and the ever-popular sexy.

That didn't leave her a lot of room for denial. So she was going to focus on being grateful for his friendship and avoid all situations that could result in him hugging her.

Sam didn't regret his promise that Faith and Phoebe could stay with him as long as they wanted. He only regretted that the temptation to kiss the sassy, sexy single mom increased in direct proportion to the number of days she'd been under his roof. It had been three nights and they were working on number four. The evacuation order was still in place because stubborn winds refused to die down. The firefighters couldn't guarantee the flames wouldn't double back and, in an abundance of caution, they were keeping everyone out. That meant there was no way to find out whether or not Faith had a home to go back to.

There was nothing to do but wait. He could tell that was easier when work kept her occupied but she was off on this hot, early August Sunday. He had a pool and her eight-year-old daughter was having a blast in it. For the better part of two hours Sam had been keeping her busy with water games to take her mind off the fire. Unfortunately it didn't take his mind off Faith, who was sitting under one of the umbrellas he'd put up poolside, pretending to read a book. Big sunglasses hid her eyes, but he was pretty sure she'd been watching him. Because she hardly ever turned a page.

"Sam, I'm going to win again." Phoebe was standing in the shallow end of the pool on the opposite side of a net he'd put up for water volleyball.

"Then you're obviously cheating."

"No, I'm not." This child could do self-righteous indignation like nobody's business. "My mom says it's wrong to cheat. Right, Mommy?"

Faith acted as if she was pulled away from the story, but the small smile on her face had been there at the cheating remark. "That's right. Connellys always play fair and cheaters never prosper."

"See?" Phoebe turned back to him, a triumphant look on her face.

"Well, if you're not cheating then I must be really bad at this game."

"You're not that bad. Maybe you just need more practice." There was an encouraging tone in her voice that was probably something she'd picked up from her mom. "I can help you anytime."

Said the child who'd declared he was important to her,

and not just because she liked his pool. "I just might take you up on that."

"If you want we could just play catch now," she offered.

"That's very nice of you."

"Mommy says we should be nice to everyone, even if they're not nice to us." She threw the ball to him.

It fell far short of his position so he moved forward. "How could anyone not be nice to you?"

"You should ask Billy Owens. He's mean."

"Who is he and what did he do?" Protective instincts Sam didn't even know he had kicked in.

"He's a boy at camp and he pulls my hair sometimes."

"Did you tell one of the camp counselors?" The phrasing of that question was so much more diplomatic than the one he really wanted to ask, which was: *Did you or someone else beat the crap out of him?*

"I talked to Miss Brenda."

"What happened?" Sam asked, holding on to the ball as he waited for an answer.

"She had a talk with him. But he did it again and called me a narc. What is a narc anyway?"

Technically it was ratting someone else out, but she had confided in a counselor which was the right thing to do. *Narc* made it ugly and he didn't want her to know about that. To stall for time, he tossed her the ball, deliberately sending it behind her so she'd have to swim for it.

"Wow, you really need practice throwing, Sam."

"I know." He saw Faith watching him, a smile on her face.

"So what happened when Billy pulled your hair again?"

"Mr. Dixon saw him do it and he had to sit on the bench when we went swimming." Her grin was filled with satisfaction, but who could blame her? "He really likes swimming in the lake."

"I'm glad he got what was coming to him." Sam lunged for the ball when she tossed it off to his right.

"And he had to say he was sorry."

"Good, the little jerk had it coming—"

"Phoebe," Faith interrupted, "you've been in the pool long enough."

"No, I haven't." There was a definite whine in her tone. "Me and Sam are having fun. And I'm helping him practice. Right, Sam?"

"You need to come out and rest." Faith saved him from getting caught in the middle. "No argument, young lady, or you will be the one sitting on the bench."

He was right. Faith had been paying attention to every word. Hopefully he'd passed inspection. After all, he'd really wanted to call that kid something far worse than jerk.

"O-okay." Phoebe dropped the ball in the water and dramatically dragged herself up the steps and out of the pool.

After wrapping her daughter in a big fluffy towel, Faith handed one to Sam.

"Thanks," he said.

"It's the least I can do since you entertained her all afternoon. I know it was to keep her from thinking about what's going on."

"Glad to help. And I didn't mind. It was fun." He dragged the thick terry cloth over his face and hair. After drying off, he pulled on his T-shirt. The sun was still high enough in the sky to get a nasty burn. "I especially liked the part where you saved me from having to explain the definition of a…" He looked at Phoebe, who was drinking the glass of lemonade her mom had put out for her. "You know."

"Yeah."

"Mom?" The little girl set the empty glass on the table beside her. She was half reclining on a lounge chair under the umbrella. "How long do I hafta rest?"

"Thirty minutes."

"But that's forever." And there was no energy behind that protest.

"I know. I'm the world's worst mother." In a low voice she added, "She'll be asleep in five minutes. And that's a good thing, what with the Sunshine Fund benefit at the community center tonight."

Sam knew all about the event to pad the town's charitable fund, because it was in an account at his bank and he managed it. And Phoebe was actually asleep in less than five minutes. "You know her pretty well."

They moved away so as not to disturb her and sat at the table underneath the patio cover.

"It's my job." She shrugged.

"You're very good at it."

"Thanks." She poured lemonade from the pitcher she'd brought outside earlier and handed him a tall glass. "You were really good with her."

"Except for the part where I wanted to run like hell when she asked what a narc is."

"Yeah. That." Faith laughed and pushed her sunglasses to the top of her head. "Seriously though, you'd be a wonderful father. Haven't you ever thought about it?"

"I'd have to be married."

"And you're really determined not to be, so some woman did you very wrong." At his questioning look she shrugged. "If you can psychoanalyze, so can I. What happened to make you so against taking that step?"

"I could ask you the same thing," he countered. "You're the one who admitted having a bad experience with love."

"I did. But I already have a child."

"And you've never mentioned her father. What's your story, Faith?" He saw a stubborn look steal into her eyes. There might not be another chance to get her to open up and he wanted her to. "How about a quid pro quo. You tell me about your bad experience and I'll share mine."

Faith met his gaze and the conflict was there in her eyes: curiosity pitted against not wanting to talk about her past. As he'd hoped, curiosity about him won out.

"You first," she said.

"Okay." He thought about where to start and decided to begin at the beginning. "My parents have a happy and loving relationship and set a high bar for what marriage should look like. So I put it off to make sure I got it right. In college I was careful not to get serious and, after graduation, I joined the family business. I developed a reputation for nerves of steel in negotiating deals."

"Obviously the other side of those deals didn't have an eight-year-old girl on the negotiating team." There was a wicked gleam in Faith's eyes.

"No." He grinned. This wasn't as hard as he'd expected. "I was professionally successful, but personally not so much. Still, corny and old-fashioned as it sounds, I wanted a marriage like my parents'. And children."

Her eyes widened. "Wait until the single ladies of Blackwater Lake hear about this."

"It's past tense. And I'm telling you this in confidence, plant lady." He waited for her to turn serious again. "Where was I? Oh, yes. The good part. I met Karen Leigh Perry at a Dallas charity event. She was beautiful, bright, funny and I fell hard. Skipping ahead, shortly after we were married, a scandal rocked the Hart family when we found out my youngest brother, Lincoln, was the result of my mother's short-term affair."

"Uh-oh."

"Yeah. Turns out the folks had problems early on. They separated and she left for a while. Cal and I were pretty young."

"Do you remember?"

"Not really. They worked things out and never talked about it. Not until Linc found out he has a different father."

"That can ruin your whole day," she said.

"More like a whole decade. It was a rough time for the Hart family." He shrugged. "But I was even more determined that my marriage would be an unqualified success. And I thought it was, so I mentioned having a baby. Karen mentioned wanting a divorce because suddenly she decided she'd never loved me."

"Oh, Sam—"

He hated the pity he saw in her eyes. That was harder than he'd expected. "It gets better. She wanted money and the divorce dragged on for a couple of years. My lawyer filed a motion and hers countered. Over and over."

"But you're divorced?"

"Oh, yes. She eventually went after Hart Industries and my family, trying to squeeze them for more money. It didn't matter that they had nothing to do with the two of us—her ruthless attorney would have used anything to get to me. At that point I just wanted it over." The bitterness was as intense now as it had been the moment he realized he had to throw in the towel. "We found a number to satisfy her and got a signature before she changed her mind. I bought and paid for the right to say "'never again.'"

"I see." Faith took a sip of lemonade. "And who could blame you?"

"I'm glad you get it."

"Just keep in mind that not all women are like that."

"'Never again' means I'll never have to find out whether or not that's true."

"By your standards it also means you'll never have children," she reminded him.

"I know." Sam was well aware. But the hit to his bank account wasn't the only casualty. His romantic notions had been pulled out by the roots and his heart poisoned. Dallas had lost its appeal and he'd needed a positive change, which was why he'd made the decision to move his corporate office to Blackwater Lake. "Your turn."

Faith sighed. "I fell in love and married my college sweetheart. After graduation we moved to Blackwater Lake where I grew up. The plan was for me to help build my aunt Cathy's florist business."

"And?" he encouraged when she stopped.

"Life was pretty perfect. I had a guy I adored and ambitious plans to expand the business." She met Sam's gaze. "Then I got pregnant."

"I don't understand. That's a good thing."

"I thought so. Dane didn't." Shadows filled her eyes. "He blamed me, said he wasn't ready for a kid. His words. He gave me an ultimatum—him or the baby. I refused to terminate the pregnancy so he terminated the marriage. He signed away his parental rights in exchange for my promise not to demand alimony or child support."

"Son of a bitch—" He stopped, glancing at Phoebe to make sure he hadn't disturbed her. She was still out like a light. And so darn cute he had to wonder what kind of a bastard could walk out on her. "Faith, I don't know what to say."

"I know the feeling." She smiled sadly.

"You should have gone after him for child support."

"I didn't want anything from a man who didn't want his own child. So I promised, and it's not my style to break my word." She shrugged.

"You are really something," he said. "Guts and resilience."

"Back at you. Giving in to the witch to protect your family. Pretty noble of you, Mr. Hart." She smiled, but it didn't warm her eyes. There was something else she wasn't saying.

"We're a pair, aren't we?" he asked.

"Mommy?" A sleepy voice came from behind them. "Can I go back in the water?"

"Duty calls." Faith got up and went to her daughter.

Sam watched the two of them and something weird knotted in his chest. He admired the hell out of this woman. She was good and kind and independent. Strong as well as sexy, and that was a pretty powerful combination. He'd liked her the first time he stopped at her flower cart in his lobby, but he liked her even more now. The fire crisis had given him the chance to know her better and he almost wished he didn't.

He *had* bought the right to say "never again" to marriage, but he'd never expected to meet a woman like Faith. But he had met her and really wanted to kiss her. He would have by now if he hadn't promised to be her friend. Crossing the line could cost him that friendship and that wasn't a risk he was willing to take.

Chapter Six

"I've been looking forward to seeing what a Blackwater Lake event looks like." Sam carried the pot of chili he'd made to the potluck table on the far wall of the community center. "I just wish it wasn't under these circumstances."

"No one wants a natural disaster," Faith agreed. "But the silver lining is that in this town, at least, it brings people closer together."

Sam nodded absently as he looked around the large rectangular room. Long portable tables were arranged in the center with folding chairs set up around them. The squares of linoleum that made up the floor were utilitarian, designed to hold up under a lot of wear and tear. At the far end of the room was a raised stage with a curtain that looked like it could be used for school or local theater productions, or just a good place to give a speech. A microphone and podium were set up in front of it now.

"There's Kayla, Mommy. Can I go see her?"

Faith set down—on a nearly full table—the casserole of

macaroni and cheese she'd made then looked in the direction her daughter was pointing. She smiled and waved at someone. "Her mom is there. Sure, sweetie, go have fun."

A young boy ran over. "Hi, Phoebe."

"Hey, Tyler. Wanna come with me and say hi to Kayla?"

"Yeah. Can I, Dad?" He looked at the tall, rugged man in a cowboy hat and boots with his arm around Kate Dixon and baby Eve. Smart money said this was her busy rancher husband, Cabot.

"Sure, Ty." The guy smiled at the dark-haired boy, then set a bowl of pasta salad on the table. "Hi, Faith. How's it going? Any word on your house?"

"Could be damaged. Could be gone." She shrugged. "Don't know yet. Thanks to Sam here, Phoebe and I have a place to live."

Cabot Dixon looked him over before holding out his hand. "Good to meet you."

"My pleasure." The man's palm was callused and worn, a sign of hard work.

"Between the Hart family moving here and Jack Garner—"

"The bestselling author?" Sam had really enjoyed his book *High Value Target*.

"That's him." Cabot pointed out a dark-haired guy with his arm around a very attractive woman. "Blackwater Lake is becoming the go-to place for the rich and famous. I know your brother, Cal, has an office here, but we haven't seen him."

"Join the club," Sam said ruefully. "He's always working. My parents joke about staging an intervention but I think my mother is starting to get serious about it."

Cabot took the fussy baby from her mother and held her high in the air, making her laugh. "It's hard to find balance. There never seems to be enough time for work and family."

"Cal isn't married," Sam said.

"If he ever surfaces from work," Kate chimed in, "there are single ladies here in town who would love an opportunity to change his status."

Sam looked at Faith and knew she was remembering their talk by the pool just a few hours ago when they each confessed their hang-ups. Now he knew she'd been burned by love just like him but that didn't make it any easier to get her off his mind. Thoughts of touching her, kissing her, were driving him nuts.

"Sam has been doing his part to uphold the Hart honor with the singles scene," Faith said. "Having my flower cart in the lobby of his building even part-time gives me a unique perspective on his perseverance in that regard."

Sam appreciated her discretion in not mentioning breakup bouquets, but he wasn't taking a chance. He steered the conversation away from himself before Kate asked any questions about his perseverance.

"There's another Hart you might not know about, because he uses his mother's maiden name. Logan Hunt is my cousin."

"I didn't know." Cabot looked surprised. "He owns the spread next to mine and I see him from time to time. The land has been in his mother's family for a couple of generations. I know him pretty well and he never mentioned a connection to the Harts."

Everyone was looking curiously at Sam, but this wasn't the time or place. And it was Logan's story to tell—if he chose to. "It's complicated," Sam said.

Before anyone could pepper him with questions, a high-pitched electronic sound made everyone in the room turn toward the microphone on stage. Mayor Goodson-McKnight stood behind the podium, presumably preparing to address the people gathered together.

"Good evening, everyone," she said. "Can you all hear me?" She looked around and seemed satisfied. "Thank you for coming to this hastily organized event to raise money for our Sunshine Fund. The Crawford's Crest fire has damaged and destroyed the homes of some of our friends and neighbors. We don't have much information yet because conditions are too volatile to safely allow anyone in. But we do know that people are going to need help to get their lives back. Thanks to everyone for coming and putting what you could into the donation jar at the door. And bringing food to share.

"Now I'd like to call someone up here so everyone can meet him. He's new to our Blackwater Lake community but clearly has the kind of spirit that will make him fit right in. This was supposed to stay between him and me, but he made an incredibly generous donation to the Sunshine Fund and it needs to be recognized. Come up here, Sam Hart, so everyone can meet and thank you."

Sam shrugged at Faith's surprised look. "She's not lying. That wasn't for public consumption."

"Way to go, Sam," Cabot said, clapping him on the shoulder.

He was reluctant to go onstage but a chant started and people stepped aside to make a path for him. There was no choice, so he joined the mayor on the raised stage. She gave him a hug and whispered, "Say a few words."

He stood behind the podium and scanned the crowd that filled the big room. "Hi, everyone. As Mayor Goodson-McKnight said, my name is Sam Hart. I know all about the Sunshine Fund because Hart Financial handles the resource distribution based on need and circumstances, with a full accounting of the dispersal to the town council. The point is, I have firsthand knowledge of how important this fund is and how it can make a difference in someone's life.

"Since I'm up here under protest, I'll take this opportunity to assure everyone that Hart Financial is here to help. Anyone whose home has been damaged or destroyed can come in with any questions about your mortgage, insurance, or even a low-interest loan to rebuild." He looked around and said, "I'm very honored to be a part of the Blackwater Lake community. Thank you."

He left the stage and walked in the general direction of where he'd left Faith. But this time his progress was slowed by men and women who stopped him to introduce themselves and shake his hand. He experienced a feeling that couldn't be put into words, a kinship that filled empty places inside him that he hadn't realized were there.

Eventually he made it back to Faith. She was still in the same spot, watching him, but the Dixons were gone.

"Look at you being all philanthropic and benevolent," she said.

"Just doing my part, ma'am."

"First of all, I'm way too young to be lumped in the *ma'am* category. Second, that must have been some big, eye-popping donation. Mayor Loretta almost never singles someone out for public adoration."

"Adoration?" he said wryly. "I didn't see any bowing. Not even a curtsy. No scraping, either. It was quite disappointing, now that I think about it."

"In their minds, people were genuflecting. Trust me. I know these things."

"You're exaggerating." Sam wasn't looking for public recognition but if Faith's estimation of him went up, he'd take it.

"I'm happy to debate the degrees of truth in my statement right after I make sure my daughter puts more than Lucy Bishop's chocolate cake on her plate."

"She makes a pretty spectacular cake, but—"

Faith lifted a finger in warning. "Before you argue that my little cherub wouldn't do that, I say she will always give it a try. It's a test to see whether or not I'm on my game."

"And in my defense, I could say that I wasn't going

to call her a cherub. Something more along the lines of 'angel.'"

"Gotcha." Faith laughed. "Am I good or what?"

Sam watched her walk away, very much appreciating the view. *Good* wasn't quite the word he would use to describe her. Witty. Perceptive. Caring and always…desirable. Wanting, sudden and powerful, slammed through him.

"So, how is it going with your house guests?"

Sam had been so captivated by Faith's assets he hadn't noticed the mayor come up beside him. He had the feeling this woman knew exactly what he'd been thinking, which was exceptionally disconcerting, considering he'd just had a visual of him, Faith, tangled legs and twisted sheets.

"What?" He forgot the question. "It's loud in here."

"I was wondering if everything is okay with Faith and Phoebe. At your house."

"Yeah. It's great having them. That little girl is something else."

"She is." The mayor smiled fondly. "I've known her since before she was born. Her aunt Cathy was my best friend. Cathy practically raised Faith, then, when she was pregnant with Phoebe, she moved back in with her."

Sam knew now that Faith had chosen her child over money and the father had willingly disappeared from his child's life before even seeing her. "If you follow an amazing kid home you usually find an amazing mom."

"You're preaching to the choir, Sam." She sighed. "She's a good person, which is why I'd like to give that weasel ex of hers a tongue lashing he'd never forget. It's not just what he did to Faith, but Phoebe, too."

"In what way? He isn't around to do anything."

"Exactly. And that absence will affect her attitudes." The mayor met his gaze. "She'll never know what a healthy relationship between a man and woman looks like."

"Faith could meet someone." Even as the words came

out of his mouth, Sam knew she'd closed that door. She'd flat-out told him so just a few hours ago. He should feel relief about her determination to stay single, not letdown about it. That would imply he might want to be the someone she met and that just wasn't the case.

"I don't think she'll ever let a man in." The older woman shook her head. "That makes me sad. Especially because I know how good it can be. My husband and I are very happy. You may not know this, but we were newlyweds not all that long ago. It took us a while to find each other."

Sam had no idea how to respond to that. "You know what? I'm starving. Being outed publicly for an anonymous donation can really give a guy an appetite."

"Okay. Let's get plates." The mayor's grin was unrepentant. "And if you were trying to scold me you should know it didn't work. The town deserved to know the truth and I'm not sorry I spilled the beans."

It was impossible to be annoyed with this straightforward woman so he let it go. Because of her, for the rest of the evening the people of Blackwater Lake walked up to shake his hand and introduce themselves. The editor of the town paper interviewed him and promised an article in the next edition so his business would get an unexpected plug.

But he probably wouldn't remember many names because he kept thinking about what the mayor had said. That little girl never had a permanent, positive male figure in her life. For as long as Faith and Phoebe were living with him, he was it, the guy who could affect her opinion—good or bad—about men.

That was a huge responsibility and he would not let her down.

Faith heard the bell above the door at Every Bloomin' Thing and knew her customer had arrived. She hurried from the office in the back to the main room with sample arrangements displayed and the cold cases keeping the flowers fresh.

Rose Hart was browsing in the shop. She was a beautiful woman with blue eyes and dark, almost black hair, here for her appointment to discuss wedding flowers. When she saw Faith, she smiled. “Hi. I hope I’m not late.”

“Right on time. Let me lock the front door and put up the closed sign so we won’t be disturbed.” Faith always tried to schedule consultations for special events at closing time to make sure all her focus was concentrated on whatever important occasion her customer was planning.

This time it was Rose. Pretty name, but Faith loved flowers and might be prejudiced. “Let’s go into my office. We can talk and figure out what you want for your wedding.”

In the back, Rose followed her past the counter with different-colored ribbon, cellophane, shears and scissors, where she worked with the flowers. On one wall, she had vases and baskets that could hold simple or sumptuous arrangements. There was a good-size room with a desk and an intimate conversation area with two comfortable chairs and a coffee table holding a couple of photo albums of her work.

Faith’s laptop was there, too. She was prepared to show examples for every occasion. Some clients preferred photographs, others were good with the electronic version.

“Have a seat.” She held out a hand, indicating the conversation area. “Can I get you something to drink? Water, soda, iced tea? Or wine?”

“Oh, wine sounds lovely. I’ve been so busy and stressed decorating the hotel. But—”

“Isn’t it a rule that a glass of chardonnay must be consumed when it’s after five and you’re planning your wedding?”

“I’m sure it must be.” Rose smiled gratefully.

"Why don't you look at my pictures. I like to show off." Faith grinned, then left her client happily perusing the albums. She walked to the back corner of the shop where she had a refrigerator. After taking out the wine bottle and opening it, she grabbed two stemmed glasses from a cupboard and poured some into them. Just a small amount for herself.

She walked back to her office and handed over one of the glasses then held up her own for a toast. "To the bride and many years of wedded bliss."

"Thank you." Rose tapped her glass to Faith's then took a sip. "I should explain that I'm not technically a bride. Linc and I are actually already married. You may have heard."

Faith nodded. "No one sneezes in this town without everyone saying God bless you."

Sam had filled in details when he told her about his witch of a wife. Lincoln Hart had eloped to Las Vegas with Rose Tucker ten years ago. His parents worked out their differences but never told him the truth about his real father. He found out and had an identity crisis, then left Rose, thinking he was protecting her from himself.

As it happened, he hired a half-priced attorney who only did half the job and never filed the divorce papers. Ten years later they were still married and in love. At least someone was getting a happy ending, Faith thought. She just hoped that if children came along there would be room in their love for someone else. That was something her own parents were unable to do for her.

"Correct me if I'm wrong," Faith said, "but this is the wedding you and Linc never had."

"Yes." The woman quite simply glowed. If happiness was electricity, she could power the lights in Blackwater Lake for a week. "Do you think I'm silly?"

"No. It's very romantic." And it was. Faith was a sucker

for romance—it was love she had a problem with. "Do you have a date picked out for the festivities?"

"Before Labor Day. I know that's not very long."

Faith already had her phone out to check for any conflict. "That works for me."

"Oh, good."

"Is there a reception?"

Rose nodded. "First event for the new hotel. They've had a soft opening and are booking guests. I've been working a lot of hours getting the lobby and banquet rooms decorated, but it's all coming together."

"Are you having attendants?"

"Yes."

Faith nodded. "Then you're going to want flowers for them to carry."

"I've asked Linc's sister, Ellie, to be my matron of honor and my best friend, Vicki, is going to be maid of honor."

"Okay. And how formal are we talking? You have to wear a long dress, veil, the whole deal?" She grinned when the other woman nodded enthusiastically. "Tuxedos for the guys?"

"Yes. Traditional."

"So you'll need a bride's bouquet." Faith tapped her lip. "Corsages for the mothers, boutonnieres for the guys and Linc's dad."

"And his biological father."

Faith's head snapped up and she studied the other woman's serene expression. "Really?"

"Yes. Linc talked to Katherine and Hastings, his parents, and they're okay with whatever he wants. Guilt could be involved, what with not telling him the truth all those years. But they seem fine with it and Linc wants the man there. Aren't we a modern family?"

"Very open-minded of everyone."

Rose smiled. "It's all good."

That was interesting, Faith thought. Sam had said his parents set a ridiculously high bar for what a happy and loving marriage should look like. It seemed they also included their four children and a biological father, too. No one was left out. Their love was a very large umbrella.

Faith had grown up with parents who didn't need anyone else, not even their daughter. She'd always felt as if she was a mistake—tick tock, the game is locked, nobody else can play. It was a lonely and confusing way to grow up.

She put the feelings aside and went through pictures, getting a feel for the bride's vision of her special day. After hearing the story about Linc showering Rose with roses to win her back, they had a theme. Roses. Long-stemmed red ones showing everlasting love for her bouquet. When she explained that lavender signified love at first sight and white signified purity the bridesmaids were taken care of.

"And the mother's corsages," Faith mused. "I happen to know your mother-in-law's favorite color is pink. Would your mom be happy with baby-pink roses?"

"She would love that."

"And I can do fishbowl arrangements of multicolored roses and baby's breath for the tables at the reception."

"Perfect." Her eyes filled with tears. "I'm sorry. I don't know why I'm so emotional."

"Don't apologize for being happy. It's just spilling over is all."

"That's a lovely way to put it." Rose brushed at the moisture on her cheeks. "Linc is excited, too. This vow renewal was all his idea."

"A Hart with a heart."

"They all have big hearts. And they'll be on display at our shindig. Although I don't know that you'll meet Cal. According to Linc he's coming but the man is dedicated to work so..." She held out her hand, rocking it back and forth. "It's anybody's guess. But Linc says a person can always count on Sam. No matter what. He's the strong, steady one."

"Is that so?"

"You don't agree?" There was a question in Rose's eyes.

"No. I mean, yes. It's just—" Faith sighed. "He's taken us in during this fire evacuation and—"

"Oh my gosh," Rose said. "Here I've been going on and on about my wedding and you're forced out of your house. I'm so sorry you're going through this."

"Thanks."

"Is there any word yet on the condition of your property?"

"Damage to the house at the very least. I don't know for sure because the fire captain hasn't let anyone back in to check. But they're getting the upper hand on it so he says it will be very soon."

"Oh, Faith—" Rose looked sincerely sympathetic. "I truly feel awful. We could have postponed this meeting about my wedding."

"That's sweet of you, but I need to be working and keeping this business going. Plus, I want everything as normal as possible for my daughter. Sam has been really good with her. Taking her mind off things whenever he can."

"You sound surprised."

"It wasn't exactly voluntary. The mayor practically twisted his arm." Faith shrugged. "Since he got roped into it, I guess I am surprised. That and the fact that he has the reputation of a serial dater."

"Is it possible that's a facade. Self-protection?"

"I get the feeling that he's perfectly happy being a yellow rose kind of guy."

"I'm sorry. What?" Rose looked confused.

"I know this about him because on first dates he gives the woman a single yellow rose, which signifies welcome without any emotional commitment."

"The thought is kind of sweet. I mean the flower part," Rose said.

"True." But Faith had sold him a whole lot of first-date flowers. "I'm sorry that's all I can tell you. Florist-client privilege prevents me from divulging details. I've already said too much."

"Wow, who knew his love life had a clandestine side." Rose was teasing, but then turned serious. "I know very little about it really, but Linc says Sam helped him through a difficult personal time. Apparently he refused to accept the label stepbrother from Linc. He said there was no 'step' about it when you love someone."

Faith had seen his rock solid character for herself. Darn it. "I suppose he's going to sprout wings pretty soon, to go along with that bright, shiny halo."

"You joke," Rose said. "And he's not perfect. But you're in good hands."

Faith got an instant visual of Sam's hands on her body in the best possible way. A shiver rolled through her and she tingled in places she had been sure would never tingle again. Any other woman would be thrilled to feel this way but Faith wasn't any woman.

She didn't need a Sam Hart pep talk. She had no doubt that he was a good guy. If she needed proof all she had to do was look at the way Phoebe reacted to him. Kids didn't suffer fools and she'd taken to him like a geek to the latest electronic device.

The fact that he was a good guy was the problem. If he was a creep she could easily ignore him. But with a man like Sam, falling in love would be so easy and she didn't want to, because it had always let her down. The emotion could make her heart write a check that her body would be only too willing to cash.

Her cell phone rang and she checked the caller ID. "It's the mayor. Do you mind?"

"Take it," Rose urged.

She hit the talk button. "Loretta, what's going on?"

"The fire captain has given the okay for you to go home."

As badly as she'd wanted to hear those words and get away from Sam, Faith was really scared.

Chapter Seven

"I'm going with you." Sam walked into Every Bloomin' Thing and made the announcement just after his sister-in-law left.

Faith slipped the strap of her purse over her shoulder. She'd just grabbed it from her office and was ready to go. "What are you talking about?"

"The evacuation order has been lifted. You're going to check out your house and I'm going with you."

Faith stared at him. "How did you find out?"

"The mayor called to give me a heads-up."

"Did she tell you to come and hold my hand?"

"No." The corners of his mouth turned up slightly. "And I'm a little hurt that you think I wouldn't come up with this idea on my own. Chivalry isn't dead, in case you wondered."

"I didn't."

"Now that I think about it, I'm miffed that you believe

I don't have the intestinal fortitude to tell Madam Mayor to take a flying leap if I felt it necessary."

"Wow, someone is feeling emotionally fragile today. What's wrong? Did the stock market take a hit?"

"Apparently not as big a ding as my ego." He didn't look hurt, just concerned.

And she was behaving like a shrew. "Look, Sam, I'm not at my best. I guess the tension is getting to me. There's a lot on my mind right now—"

"I understand. It's not necessary to say you're sorry."

"I didn't." She stood a little straighter and looked him in the eyes. "That wasn't an apology. Just giving you a frame of reference for my behavior."

"You mean being abrasive? I didn't even notice." But he nodded as if he'd already figured something out. "I'm still going with you."

"Wait. You think I was being ungracious to discourage you from coming along?"

"Something like that." He half turned toward the door. "You ready?"

No, she wanted to say. Suddenly it was all too real and wondering about the condition of her house was a more attractive prospect than actually seeing it. That didn't sweeten her disposition.

She moved closer and looked up at him. "Don't psychoanalyze me. A man who quivers with excitement over spreadsheets has no business trying to get into my head. Stick with numbers."

"Yes, statistics and figures are rational and easy to understand." He slid his sunglasses to the top of his head, revealing the sympathetic expression in his eyes. "Anyone can see what's going on—"

"I can't. Tell me," she challenged.

"You're afraid. And you're taking it out on me. I'm okay

with that. I can handle whatever you've got. My shoulders are broad."

She'd noticed, although he obviously hadn't meant that literally. But, of course, that made her look at his wide chest and muscular arms. All part of a very attractive package which aggravated her problem. "Surely you have better things to do."

"Let me be your friend. This isn't something you should do by yourself."

Since she didn't have the reserves to continue pushing back, she said, "Okay." The truth was she didn't want to do it by herself. "Phoebe's going to want to see and she should. But I need to go first so I can prepare her."

"Of course. Let's do this. I'll drive."

As they went out the door he put his hand to the small of her back. It was probably no more than an automatic gesture to him, but to Faith it was so much more. Again she felt the sweetness of not being alone. She could have and would have done this by herself but was so relieved that she didn't have to. He'd survived the shrew test.

Sam handed her into the passenger seat then he climbed behind the wheel of the SUV, which was parked in front of her shop. Her place was about fifteen minutes from town and it was a full five minutes into the drive before Faith realized he wasn't saying anything. No cheerful, meaningless words meant to make her feel better. Not even idle chitchat to distract her. She glanced over and saw that his jaw was clenched and there was a grim set to his profile.

"You're awfully quiet," she said.

"Hmm?" He glanced over. "Sorry."

"Aren't you supposed to be perky, optimistic and say stuff to keep up my spirits?"

"I would if I could think of anything inspirational to say that also happened to be true."

"Honesty from a guy is refreshing." She found it much

easier to slip into their usual banter than to speculate about what was ahead of her. "But then I'm talking to the man who sends flowers to let a girl down easy."

"Not all men are bastards."

"In case you didn't recognize it, I was paying you a compliment. We've established that you're a truthful man so obviously you believe that what you just said is true."

"I'm sensing you don't."

"I can only judge by my data. Others have different experiences. In fact your sister-in-law, Rose, is deliriously happy *now*," she said pointedly.

"Every couple has bumps." He slid her another look. "You saw Rose?"

"She left the shop just before you walked in. We discussed flowers for her renewal of vows with your brother."

"Yeah. Those two are so sweet together it makes my teeth hurt."

Faith laughed. Who knew she could do that under the circumstances? "Thank you."

"For what?"

"Not wasting your breath trying to reassure me."

"You're welcome."

Conversation stopped as they drove closer and saw signs of the recent disaster. Trunks of leafless trees were black. Bushes and shrubs had been reduced to sticks poking up through scorched ground. Structures little more than ashes with the stone chimneys as silent witnesses of what had once stood there. They passed fire department vehicles on the winding road showing they still had a presence in the area, for containment and mopping up operations.

Faith's heart squeezed painfully as her neighborhood grew closer. "All the street signs are gone."

"Yeah." Any traces of humor had disappeared from his tone.

Whole developments were wiped out. The only evidence that families had lived here were the metal remains of bicycles and cars. She knew her way without markers and gave him instructions. Sam turned onto her street and her breath caught. The houses on the side with the hill behind them were burned to the ground. But the ones on the other side were still standing, including Faith's.

But it looked like a war zone. Probably to the men and women beating back the flames it had felt that way.

"It's the one on the end." She pointed and he drove into the driveway.

When the car stopped, she jumped out and stared at what used to be her cute little house with the garden flag and pretty bushes. Sam stood beside her.

"Oh, God—" She was in shock.

There was soot and ashes everywhere, along with the overpowering stench of smoke. Trees around the property had black trunks and the bushes were trampled, but patches of grass looked salvageable. The front of the house made her stomach drop.

"It looks like the roof caught fire," Sam said.

She could see burned places as it peaked and a gap where a chunk had fallen in. All she could say was, "There's gunk all over the windows."

"My guess is that the firefighters took a stand here. The fire probably came up the hill across the street and it moved too fast to save those homes. So they lined up here and turned the hoses on the roofs."

She remembered how bad the wind had been. "In the thick of it sparks and burning pieces of whatever probably landed and took hold. So they had to water it down."

"Looks that way."

Faith walked up the sidewalk and tried to see through the windows but they were too filthy. She moved to the front door and started to turn the handle, then remembered it was locked. When she'd left, everything had been perfectly normal and now—it wasn't.

"I'm going to get my key." Because it seemed wrong to do more damage and break a window she thought. How absurd.

"I don't think it's a good idea to go in. The roof is unstable. And it should be inspected before anyone goes inside."

"I'll just look—" Emotion choked off her words. She fished keys out of her purse and unlocked the door then pushed it wide.

The smoky odor was even stronger and smelled like the remains of a campfire doused by water. She could see into the dining and family rooms and part of the kitchen. Not an inch of it was untouched. The furniture was dirty and waterlogged, the walls dingy with soot.

She was too shocked even to cry. "Where do I start? How am I going to tell Phoebe? I don't even know when we can come back."

"Okay. Now it's time for reassuring words. And you know I'll tell you the truth." Sam put his arm around her shoulders. "It's not a total loss, which is something. A building inspector can tell us for sure if the foundation and frame are sound, which I think they are. So that will speed up repairs. Plus I have connections in the construction business. My sister is an architect. More important, her husband is a contractor. And finally, the bank has resources in addition to the money that the state of Montana and the federal government will make available to victims since it was declared a disaster area." He slid his sunglasses to the top of his head, letting her see the confidence in his expression. "And I meant what I said. You and Phoebe can stay with me as long as you need to."

"Oh, Sam—" She threw herself against him and hugged for all she was worth.

When his arms came around her it was natural and

right. She'd never felt so safe in her life. Not with her parents who were too wrapped up in their love for each other to pay much attention to her. And definitely not with her husband. The jerk. Sam Hart didn't just talk the talk. He walked the walk.

And again she was overwhelmed, this time by gratitude. He'd been discussing the situation in terms of "we" and "us," as in being with her while she was going through the process of getting her life back. He was strong, reassuring her with words but mostly just by holding her. The desire to stay right where she was forever overwhelmed her, compelling enough that she forced herself to pull away. So much for avoiding hugging situations.

But he only wanted to be her friend; she couldn't let him see that she'd felt much more just now.

"Don't worry, Faith. I know it doesn't look good at this moment, but everything will be okay." There was a sheepish expression on his face. "Sorry. That was the best I could do for a perky, inspirational speech. Did it get your spirits up?"

She smiled—it was wobbly but she managed. "Thank you for being such a good *friend*."

"You're welcome." But his eyes darkened with intensity that looked like much more than friendly.

She didn't know what to do with that information.

The day after seeing Faith's house, Sam sweet-talked his sister, Ellie, into inviting the three of them to dinner. It didn't take much arm-twisting when he explained about telling Phoebe she wouldn't be going back to her house for a while. His sister picked up on the fact that the little girl could use a distraction and her daughter, Leah, could provide that.

He knew Ellie and her husband, Alex, would want to pitch in and help with repairs however they could. So here they were, eating hamburgers and hot dogs in the McKnights' backyard. They were sitting around a circular table with four small benches—Ellie and Alex on one, Phoebe and Leah side by side, and he and Faith. Every cloud had a silver lining, and his was that they were here to manage her crisis, but his shoulder constantly brushed up against hers. He liked it. So sue him.

Ellie frowned at her daughter, who had flatly refused a booster chair because she wanted to sit like "Bebe." Almost-three-year-olds didn't always get words or names right but Phoebe wasn't phased at all. She thought little Leah was the cutest thing ever. Sam agreed, although it was a toss-up when you put Phoebe in the mix. But his niece wasn't eating and her mother wasn't happy about it.

"You know, Ellie," Sam said, "this taking a stand about a clean plate is seriously cutting into my niece's play time."

"Phoebe," Faith said, "maybe you can make a game of it. You take a bite, then Leah can."

"Okay, Mom." Phoebe smiled at the little dark-haired girl next to her on the picnic bench. "Leah, want to play a game?"

"Yes!"

"I had no idea she knew that word," Ellie said drily. "All I hear is no."

"Let's see who can finish their hot dog first," Phoebe said. "Go."

"Wow." Ellie watched the two girls chow down. "If only she was that cooperative with me. Especially at bedtime. I want Phoebe to live here."

"I'd miss her terribly." Faith laughed. "How about I send her here when she's being difficult?"

"I'll take that deal." Ellie made a face when Leah shoved a piece of hot dog into her mouth. "Phoebe, will you please tell her to chew?"

"Okay, Mrs. McKnight." She looked at the child. "Chew like this, Leah."

The little girl perfectly imitated what she was shown and cleaned her plate, then held it up for her parents' approval.

Alex smiled proudly. "Way to go, baby girl."

"Not baby." His daughter gave him a look.

"And there it is," Sam observed. "I didn't realize it started so young."

Ellie looked at her child, then back to him. "What?"

"The universal female expression that requires no translation. But let me attempt it. Without a word, she said you just don't understand," he told his sister. "You're a dolt and possibly too stupid to live. You should be squished like a bug. I wonder if it started during caveman days and the women looked at Ug dragging home a woolly mammoth and he got the look. The one that said, 'Really, that's all you've got for dinner? We need berries and poison ivy to balance that into a meal.'"

Ellie and Faith were laughing hysterically, but Alex was nodding, complete understanding.

"How do I tell her she'll always be my baby girl?" he asked.

Sam happened to be looking sideways at Faith just then and saw her smile disappear. He could almost read her mind, see the regret that her little girl's father hadn't wanted her. Again, he felt the determination to show Faith that not all men walked out on their responsibilities. Most guys were reliable and Sam was one of them. She could come to him for anything and he would be there.

"She doesn't have to understand it, Alex," he said. "She just needs to know her dad always has her back."

"Aww, Sam..." Ellie sniffled a little. "I had no idea you were so sweet and perceptive."

Basking in her praise, he took a sip of his beer then set the bottle down. “Don’t sound so surprised.”

“Can’t help it. You were such a toad when we were growing up,” she teased.

“My life would have been easier if he’d stayed a toad.” Alex looked ruefully at Sam. “When I wanted to marry your sister, I had to go through all of her siblings.”

“What are big brothers for?” Sam would do it again. “It was a test and you passed.”

“In all fairness, Alex, you were being kind of a toad yourself during that time. Don’t pout.” Ellie put her head on his shoulder. “You became my McKnight in shining armor.”

“That’s so adorable,” Faith said.

“Mommy, me play Bebe?”

Ellie inspected her clean plate. “You may be excused.”

Apparently Leah understood because she scrambled off the bench, her mother’s hand hovering close by in case she needed help.

“Bye,” Leah said to the adults in general. “Bebe, go play?”

Phoebe looked at her mom. “Can I?”

“Yes, you *may*.”

The little girl rolled her eyes in the universal language of a kid whose grammar was just corrected for the umpteenth time. This was training for the teenage years. Right now she was just a kid who ran after another kid. Girlish giggles ensued along with screeching at a pitch only dogs could hear. But the happy scene touched something inside Sam.

It was a feeling he’d had once before that had gone terribly wrong and left him even more alone. Asking for a child had been the end of his marriage and the beginning of the hell it would take to legally make her go away. He hadn’t thought about children of his own again. Until now.

Watching the girls play made him realize the deep, primal emotion had never gone away. He wanted one of those small humans.

"They can't get to the pool, right?" Faith was critically considering the high fence around it. "Phoebe can swim but—"

"Don't worry," Alex assured her. "Leah is in water safety lessons. But they'd have to be Houdini to get in there. The fencing was designed by my talented and overprotective wife and the crew put it in to my specifications. You probably know I'm in construction."

"Thanks for the segue," Sam said. "Faith could use your help."

Ellie was stacking paper plates. "I didn't want to bring it up in front of Phoebe. How did she take the news?"

"Pretty well." Faith glanced at him. "Sam really helped."

"My brother? No way," Ellie scoffed. "Who'd have thought?"

"He told her the truth and what to expect. That after it's inspected and judged safe, we'll go see what we can salvage. She, of course, was thinking toys."

"How is the house?" Alex asked.

"The roof needs replacing for sure," Faith told him. "Walls look to be in okay shape, but parts are scorched. There's water damage."

"Probably wallboard will have to be removed down to the studs." Alex took a sip of his beer and thought for a few moments. "Sam is right. Safety first, then see what can be saved, clothes, toys, kitchen stuff. My guess is the furnishings are gone and will have to be disposed of. After packing up what's salvageable and trashing the rest, demolition can start."

"I have a thought," Ellie chimed in. "It kind of comes under the heading of when life gives you lemons—"

"Make lemonade?" Alex finished. "What are you thinking, honey?"

"Look at it as an opportunity to make some changes. Improvements and updating. Unless you thought it was perfect just the way it was."

"No." Faith laughed but there was no humor in the sound. "It's an older home and could use some modernizing, but..."

"What?" Sam encouraged.

"I'm sure there would be added cost."

He knew where she was going with this. "You have homeowner's insurance."

"Yes, but there's a deductible."

He was ready for that. "Like I said, there's government disaster money and the Sunshine Fund."

"That will probably get it back to the way it was," she acknowledged. "But from a financial perspective, I can't afford to do more than that."

"Think of it as an investment." Sam really wanted something good to come out of this for her. "It will add value to the property."

"Spoken like a numbers guy." There was defeat in her voice that was uncharacteristic of the feisty plant lady.

Sam had an intense desire to fix that, probably because she fought so hard to be independent. Earlier he'd convinced her to let him be her friend and support her through a first look at the damage to her house. Then she'd thrown herself into his arms and the urge to protect her had been overwhelming. And still was.

"Value is important," he said. "But you also need to be happy."

"I'd love that but it always comes back to the cost." She was trying to act tough, but it was easy to see through that and how upset she really was. Reading between the lines, she was saying it was not in the budget of a single woman who was raising a daughter.

Sam only wanted to make her world right again. "I'll loan you the money. Interest-free."

Her gaze snapped to his. "What?"

"I have it. Let me help.

"It's my problem, I'll handle it. But thank you."

"That's it?" Sometimes, he thought, her pigheadedness was incredibly frustrating. "You won't even think over the offer? I thought we were friends."

"We are. And I value that too much to take a loan from you. It's practically guaranteed to destroy that relationship. Money is the root of all evil. You should know that."

"And why is that?"

"Look what happened with your ex-wife." She glanced at Ellie, who was nodding.

Sam frowned at her, the expression guaranteed to reduce anyone to quivering compliance. "I'm sorry I told you about that."

"I'm not. It's good information to have. Forewarned is forearmed and all that."

She was putting up walls, which was pretty infuriating. And ironic since the walls of her house literally had to be put up. "Alex, you have connections. Can you get an inspector to Faith's house tomorrow?"

"Really, Sam?" Ellie's tone was teasing. "You're in quite a hurry. You must really want Faith and Phoebe out of your place pronto."

"No. My house is their house as long as they need it." He shrugged and met Faith's gaze. "I just want to help make her life whole again."

"And it's much appreciated," she said, smiling a little.

But there was something in her eyes, a sad expression that he hadn't seen before. During their quid pro quo by his pool, he'd had the feeling there was something she wasn't telling him about her past.

Sam was determined to find out what because he wanted to know everything about her. After he got her safely back into her renovated home maybe this blasted protective streak would go away.

Chapter Eight

Several days after the barbecue with his sister, Sam drove beneath the Dixon Ranch sign again but this time he was alone. He pulled the car to a stop by the ranch house as he had before and found Cabot Dixon himself on the porch holding his daughter. Sam parked the SUV and got out, then walked up to the rancher and shook the man's hand.

"Good to see you again, Cabot."

"You, too." He shifted the wiggly little girl to his other arm. "Faith called and said you'd be picking Phoebe up today."

"Yeah. She's meeting my brother-in-law at her house so he can assess the damage and come up with a plan for repairs."

"How bad is it?"

"Frankly, it's a miracle that anything is left up there." Sam dragged his fingers through his hair. "The street signs are all burned and twisted metal. That's one reason she had to go with Alex, to show him where it is. Across the street from her place, everything is gone. You can see the outlines of foundations but ashes are all that's left. The bad news is her house isn't fit to live in right now."

"Thanks to you, she doesn't have to worry about where she's going to stay."

"Just doing my civic duty." Although he was pretty sure the definition of "civic" didn't include wanting to kiss Faith and make her clothes fall off. "Trying to be a part of this town. Neighborly spirit. Doing my share to pitch in…"

The other man half smiled, as if he could read minds. "You're sure that's all there is to it?"

"Yeah." Sam knew brotherly concern when he saw it. He'd almost convinced himself that his feelings for her fell into that category, then she'd hugged him at the house. It had only been gratitude on her part but for some reason his body hadn't received that message.

"How's she holding up?" When his daughter fussed, Cabot lifted her high over his head to get a laugh.

"Amazingly well. She's a strong woman." He noticed that the other man was looking thoughtful. "Something wrong?"

"Probably not. But it's traumatic for the whole family."

"You mean Phoebe."

Cabot nodded. "One of the camp counselors mentioned in the daily report that she's been unusually quiet. Who could blame her?"

"Yeah. Faith tried to break the news gently, but now she knows she's not going home right away. I'll talk to Faith about it."

"Good. I thought it's something she should be aware of."

"Here comes Phoebe now." Sam spotted her walking up the dirt path from the lake where most of the camp activities took place.

Was it his imagination after what Cabot had said, or were her shoulders slumped and her steps dragging? From the first day she and her mom came to stay with him a few weeks ago, Phoebe had been lively, energetic, outgoing. Chatty. Maybe she wasn't dejected, just tired.

"Hey, Squirt," he said when she stopped beside him. "I volunteered to pick you up today."

"I know. Can we go now?"

"Sure." This was a very different child from the one he had seen this morning. He glanced at the rancher and saw the man frown. He'd seen it, too. "Good to see you, Cabot."

"Say hi to Faith for me."

"Will do."

He and Phoebe walked to the car and he took the pink backpack before opening the front passenger door. Then he remembered something Ellie had said about kids and cars. "Do you need one of those booster things to sit on? Can you ride in the front seat or do you have to be in the back facing the rear?"

Phoebe gave him the are-you-that-dense look. "I'm not a baby, Sam. And I'm tall enough to sit in front. My weight is okay for the seat belt to be safe. Mom checked."

"I bet she did. Okay then." He was way behind the learning curve. This role-model, watching-over-an-eight-year-old-girl duty was a tough gig. There was a lot to remember.

Sam waited for her to climb in then closed the door. It was on the tip of his tongue to say she should always insist that a guy be a gentleman and open doors for her. Maybe that was jumping the gun, but he didn't know how long he'd be around to give her the scoop on boys.

He got in the driver's side and started the engine. "Is there anywhere you want to go?"

"No."

Sam glanced over at her before driving back the way he'd come. Her voice was flat, lacking the normal energy and high spirits. "Did you have a good day?"

"It was okay."

He waited for more that didn't come. "What did you do?"

"Stuff."

"Did you swim?" he asked.

"Yes."

He was running out of conversation starters. Granted, he didn't speak fluent eight-year-old but it was obvious even to him that she was having an off day. Maybe she just needed some space.

Neither of them spoke the rest of the way home and Sam became increasingly uneasy. He'd bet his beloved big-screen TV that something bad was going on. Still, he was completely out of his depth here and leaning toward staying out of it, erring on the side of not making things worse. Let her mom handle it when she got home. But…

There was always a but. That was a powerful word and could stop something or start it. Potential good or possible disaster. Since the night of the Sunshine Fund benefit he had been acutely aware of the whole role model, responsibility thing. Maybe giving her space was a mistake.

Her father had given her space and now there was a hole in her life that needed to be filled. Even if it was by an amateur who was only temporary.

After hitting the button on the garage door opener, he drove the car into its place of honor and turned off the engine. He got out and opened Phoebe's door before retrieving her backpack from the rear seat. They walked inside, Phoebe preceding him.

Sam hung her backpack on the stairway post and said, "Do you want something to eat? We can fix it together."

"I'm not hungry."

"Not even for pancakes?" Sam knew she was really a big fan of those.

"That's for breakfast." Not even a glimmer of her normal spunky personality.

"Your stomach doesn't care about that," he said.

"My tummy feels funny." She looked more than a little pathetic.

"Are you sick?" He put his hand on her forehead. Why? Must have been what his mom did when he was a kid.

"No. Can I go to my room now?"

"Sure, but..." There was that word again. "First I'd really like you to tell me what's bothering you."

"I don't want to talk about it."

Sam might be a beginner but he recognized that she didn't give him the typical female response that she was fine. So there was something not right. "It might help to get it off your chest."

"It won't."

"How do you know?"

"Talking doesn't do any good." It sounded as if she'd tried dialogue without results. Worse, she wouldn't look at him.

"Telling me might make your tummy feel better."

"Nothing will help."

"Are you sure? You won't know unless you try." He angled his head toward the family room. "Let's sit down and give it a shot." He put his hand gently between her shoulder blades, not nudging but just to let her know that he was there. If she shut him down he wasn't sure what else to do. So it was a relief when she sighed and moved toward the corner group in front of the TV.

"What's up?" he asked, sitting beside her.

"There's a girl at camp. She's boarding there all summer." Phoebe glanced up for a moment. "She's being mean to me."

"I see." He didn't at all. He was pissed. But on some level it registered that letting her know would be unhelpful. "How is she being mean?"

"She makes fun of me in front of other kids." She sounded so small and vulnerable.

That made Sam want to put his fist through the wall, but again it would only make him feel better and probably scare Phoebe. He blew out a breath. "Have you asked her to stop?"

"Yes. My mom always says to use words but that's not working. It just makes her do it more. And I can't tell my mom because she'll worry."

Sam's state of pissed-off-ness went up a notch. This was bullying. If she'd been a boy he would have known what to say but she was a girl. His need to Google anti-bullying techniques bordered on desperation because now Phoebe was looking at him as if he had all the answers. God help him.

Numbers on a spreadsheet were useless to him at this moment, which was too bad because he'd give anything to fix Phoebe's problem. What would Faith do?

"Have you told your camp counselor what's going on?" he asked.

"No. That would be tattling."

And left the tattler open to retaliation. "Has this girl ever pushed you or—?"

Phoebe shook her head. "She likes to make the other kids laugh and makes fun of my clothes and hair."

So for now it wasn't a physical threat, not that he felt any less angry while this child was suffering emotional abuse. But thoughtful intervention was appropriate. The kid tormenting Phoebe was trying to be cool in front of her peers, to elevate her own status at Phoebe's expense.

"It sounds to me as if she's putting you down to make herself feel better."

"I guess." Slim shoulders rose for a moment, then fell.

"You have lots of close friends there. Does she do it when they're around?"

The little girl thought for a moment, then looked up. There was a speck of hope in her eyes. "No."

"Then it seems to me you should try to avoid her and make sure you're with one or more of your friends. If she tries they'll stick up for you. Right?"

"I think so."

"Good." This had to be said. "If that doesn't work, Mr. Dixon and your camp counselor should know what's going on. So they can talk to her." Sam knew Faith needed to make the decision on that because there could be unpleasant consequences for her daughter.

The little girl sat up straighter and met his gaze. "Tyler Dixon is my friend. And he's older. She never says anything bad when he's around. She always smiles at him."

The shrew-in-training had a crush on the rancher's son, he realized. Best to keep that information to himself. "Then you're probably going to want to hang out with Tyler. And remember, Phoebe, camp is almost over. That girl will go back where she came from and school will start where all your friends are. But you should enjoy the rest of your summer. If the situation makes you unhappy or uncomfortable, you can't keep it to yourself. There are people to help. Mr. Dixon, your mom. And me—"

"I'll remember." She smiled then.

Sam felt the weight of the world lift from his shoulders and smiled back. "I don't know about you, but in my opinion this was a good talk."

She nodded, then without warning threw herself into his arms. "I love you, Sam."

When he could get words past the lump in his throat, he said, "Back at you, Squirt."

"I'm hungry. Can we have pancakes for dinner?"

"Anything you want."

And he meant that. This kid had him completely hooked. How could a father just leave her? That was his loss, because she was terrific and so was her mom. It was a damn shame that the man who should have been there for both of them had taken from Faith—well, her faith.

She wasn't ever going to trust a man again and anyone who made the mistake of falling for her would suffer the consequences. Sam had already been burned by consequences of his own and once was more than enough.

Faith was tired to the bone.

She'd met Alex at the house and he was going to arrange for the building inspector to check it out, but warned that with so much property damage from the fire there was going to be a long line. He recommended patience. *Good luck with that*, she thought.

She'd missed dinner and now had to put on a brave, cheerful face for Phoebe. That thought just made her want to curl into the fetal position. Since she was behind the wheel of her van, that would be a problem for other drivers on the road. A few minutes later she parked her car in front of Sam's house and used the key he'd given her to get in the front door.

"I'm home."

That was automatic and she wanted the words back because this wasn't their home. It was beautiful and big and she really loved the place, but it wasn't where she belonged. Right now she felt as if they would never again have a home and it took so much energy to keep Phoebe from seeing.

"Hi, Mommy." The little girl came running to meet her in the family room and threw herself into Faith's arms.

She hugged her child close and was a little surprised when her daughter didn't pull away instantly. "Hello, baby girl."

"I'm not a baby." Phoebe looked up and grinned before stepping back.

"You sound like Leah."

"Don't let my niece hear you say that." Sam stood with his back to the kitchen island. "Hi."

"Hey."

This was when it really sucked to be so tired. He looked sinfully masculine and sexy with one ankle crossed over the other. It was starting to be a habit but that didn't stop Faith from wanting to throw herself into his arms and not let go. He might even rub her back and whisper to her that everything would be okay. And she might even pretend to believe him because of how much she wanted it to be true.

If she was very lucky he might even kiss her.

"Faith?"

"Hmm?"

"I asked how it went with Alex. At the house," he added, as if recognizing her brain blip.

"Good."

"Can we go home, Mom?"

"Not yet. And it's hard to say when." She pulled the little girl close to her side and willed an optimistic tone into her voice. "It's like four hundred thirty-two things have to happen and we're at number five. But soon we'll have a plan."

"Waiting is the hardest part," Sam said softly.

Apparently he saw right through her stiff-upper-lip routine. There was sympathy bordering on pity in his eyes, Faith realized.

"Yeah." What else could she say when he was right?

"Did you eat?" he asked.

"No, but I don't really feel like it. My stomach—" She put a hand to her abdomen where there was a knot the size of a Buick.

"Do you want to talk about it, Mom?" Phoebe had such a wise, mature look on her little face.

"No, sweetie, that's okay."

"Sam said talking would make my tummy feel better and he was right."

"Really?" Faith noticed the glimmer in his eyes and tried to decide whether it was self-satisfaction or humor.

"I can make you pancakes," he offered.

"They were so good, Mom. Sam said my tummy wouldn't care if it wasn't breakfast time and it didn't. I really liked them for dinner."

Sam studied her a little warily. "I also grill a mean cheese sandwich. It pairs well with a light, crisp chardonnay."

"You had me at 'sandwich.'" And suddenly Faith was starving. "But I wouldn't say no to a glass of wine."

"Coming right up."

She and Phoebe watched him assemble a pan, bread, cheese and everything he would need. Then Faith noticed the digital readout on the microwave clock.

"Phoebe, it's time for your shower. You have to get up early for camp tomorrow."

"Do I have to?"

Faith heard something in her voice and saw rebellion in her eyes. Connecting that and the comments about Sam being right, she had a feeling something was up. "I'm sorry, kiddo. You do have to, but I'll come up and help."

"That's okay. I can do it." Phoebe dragged herself dramatically out of the room.

When she started to follow, Sam said, "Can I talk to you first?"

"Okay." The Buick knot was back. "What's going on?"

"Cabot said one of the camp counselors noted that she was unusually quiet today. I thought it might be because of the fire damage to her house. Even to a rookie like me it was obvious that she was bummed when I picked her up. Eventually I convinced her to tell me why." He took a spatula from the drawer by the stove. "A girl at camp is giving her a hard time."

"Bullying?"

"Classic definition of it. I looked it up." His expression turned sheepish. "Don't judge. I was flying by the seat of my pants."

She couldn't suppress a small smile, but it didn't last long. "She hasn't said anything to me."

"She didn't want you to worry."

Faith was annoyed, frustrated and proud all at the same time. "Okay."

"I thought you should know."

"Good call." In a nanosecond house worries shrank in importance. Funny how concern for your child's emotional welfare could take your mind off dealing with fixing the roof over your heads. "I appreciate the information, Sam."

She hurried up the stairs and passed the bathroom, where the shower was already on. After putting out pink pajamas, she went in to help. Steam filled the room.

"Doing okay, Phoebs?"

"Yes."

Faith leaned a shoulder against the wall while she waited and let her throbbing pulse slow down. "Did you go swimming today?"

"Yes."

"Then you have to wash your hair."

"I know."

This ritual was so routine. They did this every night, except the part where Faith wanted to fire questions at her like a prosecuting attorney in court. But she held back and forced herself to make meaningless conversation. It took every ounce of her willpower not to demand the name of the twerp who hurt her.

Finally the water turned off, and when the shower curtain was pushed back, Faith wrapped her in the big fluffy towel then used a brush to untangle the long blond strands. A few minutes later she was in her jammies and climbing into the big bed, in the beautiful room under Sam Hart's roof. And someone at the summer camp that was supposed to be fun had tormented her child.

Faith sat on the edge of the mattress and smiled before saying what she always said during the bedtime ritual. "Tell me about your day."

"Not good."

"What happened?" Faith's chest tightened.

"Shelby Finch made fun of my shirt and shorts. She said they were ugly."

Faith wanted to ask if Shelby Finch had been forced to evacuate her house with nothing but the clothes on her back. Did she have to cobble together a wardrobe on a shoestring budget because everything she owned was threatened by a wildfire? Instead Faith said, "That's not very nice."

"I know. I talked to Sam about it."

"That's good." Faith would have loved to have been a fly on the wall and eavesdropped on that conversation.

"He said I should stay away from her and hang out with my friends. Because she only does it when I'm all by myself."

"That sounds like a pretty good idea." She brushed the hair out of Phoebe's eyes. "It won't be long until camp is over and Shelby will go home." Good riddance to the little dweeb.

"That's what Sam said." Phoebe yawned. "Mommy, can Sam pick me up again tomorrow?"

"Oh, honey, he's already doing so much by letting us stay here. We shouldn't impose on him."

The little girl rolled to her side and looked up sleepily. "I think it would be okay because he likes us."

"He's being a good neighbor."

"But he's different from most grown-ups. They don't always pay attention to kids." Her eyes closed.

"I know. And they should. Good night, baby girl." No pushback on the endearment meant that she was well on her way to being sound asleep.

Faith kissed her forehead, then tucked the covers snugly around the little body and turned off the bedside lamp. Quietly she left the room and went downstairs.

She was sort of getting used to feeling overwhelmed in ways both good and bad. What Sam had done for her little girl fell into both positive and negative territory. She walked into the kitchen, where he was standing at the stove, watching over a sandwich he was grilling for her. There was a glass of wine on the counter and he picked it up then handed it to her.

"Thank you. And—" She shook her head as emotion flooded her. "There are no words to express my gratitude."

"I just opened the bottle and poured. It was no big deal," he teased.

"Not that." She met his gaze. "You took the time to listen to a child who was going through something traumatic."

His expression turned grim. "Do you have any idea how hard it is to just listen when all you want to do is fix the problem?"

"Yes, I do, actually." She wanted to say *Welcome to the hood—parenthood.* But he wasn't Phoebe's father. Just a guy doing a favor, being neighborly.

"She's concerned about being a snitch, which I can respect. So we brainstormed some ideas for her to deal with the situation on her own. But after talking over strategies I warned her that the people in charge of the camp might need to know what's going on."

"Sound advice." She sipped her wine. "And they're going to. If not before, then on the last day I intend to talk to Cabot about that little girl. In case he wants to turn down her application next summer. He always has a waiting list."

"Excellent." Sam lifted his beer bottle in salute.

Faith leaned a hip against the cupboard beside him. "I'm a little surprised you didn't recommend that Phoebe pull that little witch's hair or something even more physical."

"You have no idea how hard it was not to." He stood there in his snug, worn jeans and equally formfitting T-shirt looking right at home cooking. Why in the world was that the sexiest thing ever? "I'm a novice, but something told me you'd frown on that."

"Unfortunately, that's a yes. You did good, Sam. Thank you—" When tears unexpectedly filled her eyes she was completely mortified. After setting her glass on the counter beside her, she brushed the tears away. "I'm s-sorry—"

He moved close enough for her to feel the heat from his body. "I've already been thanked. Phoebe gave me a hug. I think she likes me."

She wasn't the only one, Faith thought. "You're very good with her. And I appreciate that more than you can possibly know. I didn't mean to get all blubbery and make you uncomfortable."

Gently, Sam reached out and cupped her cheek in his big hand, brushing a tear away with his thumb. "Never apologize for loving your child that much."

Faith's heart skipped at the intensity in his eyes and she held her breath. He was going to kiss her. Anticipation grew inside her as she waited to see what his mouth would feel like against her own. He lowered his head and tingles danced over her skin as time seemed to slow. Then he pressed his lips to her forehead. She'd never had a brother but would swear that was the way one would have behaved with his sister.

Sam moved away and flipped the sandwich in the pan

to brown the other side and melt the cheese. He should be good at that, what with the way he'd melted her insides.

Well, on the up side, she wasn't crying anymore. But now she was confused and distressed in equal parts. She'd thought he was going to kiss her. Could she really have been so wrong? By far her strongest emotion was disappointment that he hadn't followed closely by the certainty that if Sam ever made a move on her, she would definitely *not* push him away.

Chapter Nine

Sam was at loose ends and had too much time to think. That was never a good thing.

In a couple hours his brother was getting married, or re-vowing, as he and Rose were calling it. Sam had badly wanted to needle Linc about whether or not a second wedding meant more than one divorce if things went south. Two things stopped him. Linc wasn't the least bit nervous about the ceremony. In fact he couldn't wait. And he'd been in love with Rose for ten years. They were lucky and Sam envied them. But he was still bored.

Everyone in the wedding party had been ordered to show up at Holden House several hours before the ceremony, dressed and ready to rock and roll. April Kennedy, the town photographer, was taking pictures and had finished with the men. It was the ladies' turn and they could be tied up right until the ceremony. Linc was with his two dads and that was too weird for Sam. So he was wandering around by himself, checking out the brand-new hotel.

That was when he spotted Faith wheeling a flat cart of flower-filled vases and supplies into the Mountain View Room, where the vows were going to take place. Talking to her was never boring, so he pushed open the door where she'd just disappeared. She was setting flower arrangements on either side of the hearth in front of a river rock fireplace with a cherrywood mantel. It was decorated with garlands of greens and flowers across the top that draped down the side to the floor. Rows of chairs were set up facing it.

"Hi," he said, walking closer.

Faith gasped and whirled around, then pressed a hand to her chest when she recognized him. "My God, Sam. You startled me."

"Sorry. I thought you heard me." Although he was impressed by her focus on the job. He couldn't help wondering if her concentration extended to other, more personal activities.

Such as kissing. And sex.

Those two endeavors had been high on his try-not-to-think-about list since the night over a week ago when she'd thanked him for listening to Phoebe. The sweet torture of her breasts against his chest had made his hands ache to feel her soft, bare skin. And all of her feminine curves nestled close to him had made it damn near impossible to remember he was trying not to cross that line with her.

"What are you doing here?" Faith asked.

"I thought the tuxedo was a big clue, but that could just be me."

"If that's an attempt to reinforce your ego, I'll play along. You look very handsome." When she glanced up, there was a glimmer of appreciation before it vanished. Then she was back to concentrating as she knelt by a chair and fastened a three-dimensional white bow, a rose and baby's breath to it.

"Thank you."

"I know there's a wedding," she said wryly. "My point is, don't you have somewhere to be? Something to do before it starts?"

"No." He slid his hands into the tailored black Armani trousers that matched the jacket. By his count there were fifty chairs. Not that he was a mathematical genius, but there were ten rows with five across. And she was just starting. "I am useless."

"Like a bump on a pickle."

"Exactly."

She twisted some wire, then expertly tucked it out of sight before moving sideways and starting the same routine on the next chair. "Surely someone needs you."

"Sadly, no."

"What about pictures?" With speed and skill she worked to attach the flowers and bow before again moving on.

"Already done." He followed behind her, watching her slender, delicate hands work magic. What if she touched him?

She stopped suddenly and looked up at him. "You okay, Sam?"

"Fine." Unless you factored in that he had probably made some sort of sound and tipped her off to his internal conflict about her.

She returned her attention to what she'd been doing. "Did April take more than one picture?"

"Of course. But we're men. No one cares about us. I probably won't even make the cut for the album."

"Why not? You're the groom's brother after all."

"Which is the only reason I'm in the wedding party at all. Other than that, I'm nothing. Just a suit to escort women down the aisle to their seats."

"Not the best man?" Faith glanced up.

"At this shindig? Not a chance."

"Who is? Your brother Cal?"

"Oh, please… My parents are just happy he showed up."

"Rose told me he works a lot," she said.

"Yeah. And it requires traveling. He's the CEO of Hart Energy and is off looking at alternative energy sources that have minimal environmental impact. The latest one is algae."

"Sounds like a worthy business enterprise."

"More like an excuse for a getaway to somewhere remote and exotic."

"So you think he's a slacker?"

Sam laughed. "Cal is many things, but that's not one of them. If anything he's an adventurer, but definitely he works too much."

"So he's not in the wedding because he could have been a no-show. That's what Rose told me."

"Right," he confirmed.

"Who is the best man?"

"My dad." Sam smiled at the memory of Linc asking Hastings to do the honors. It was the first time he'd ever seen his father quite so emotional.

Faith studied his reaction. "What?"

She was progressing with this task at a pretty good clip and he moved with her to the next chair. "It's just… That was a moment, when he asked dad."

"Why?"

"There was tension between them when Linc found out Hastings isn't his biological father."

"I heard about that."

"Oh?"

"Like I told Rose, the only way to keep a secret in this town is to not tell anyone." She must have seen that he was still surprised because she added, "We discussed it when she came in for flowers. I had to know how many boutonnieres to make."

"She certainly shared a lot of information."

"True, but the best man selection was something she kept to herself."

When she started to stand, he held out his hand. "Allow me."

She hesitated a fraction of a second, then accepted his assistance. The feel of those graceful fingers in his palm was like sparks on dry grass, threatening to consume him. Suddenly his starched white collar was too tight and he couldn't breathe.

"Thanks." Her voice was a little strained and she snatched her hand away as if it burned. "Now I have to do the chairs on the other side."

"Do you mind if I keep you company?"

"No." She moved toward the end chair in the front row. "But you're sure your brother doesn't need you?"

"If he does, it's only because he's stuck with his two dads."

"At the same time?" Her eyes widened before crouching down to work. "Awkward?"

"I would think so."

"Me, too."

Sam stood by the chair she'd finished and watched her move efficiently down the row. "But I guess the three of them are okay."

"How can you tell?"

"Because I haven't heard anything. They never call. Never text."

"You're making fun," she said, "but I think it's wonderful that everyone has put aside their differences and are getting along. For Linc and Rose."

"We're a regular modern family," he said wryly.

"That's what she said. I don't know about modern." Faith was working on the last chair. "But you're all here."

This time when Sam helped her to her feet he saw shadows in her eyes. "It's understood that we show up. We're related."

"It's more than that, Sam. You all care enough about each other to be present for the happy stuff. And even when things aren't so happy."

What was going on in that head of hers? he wondered. He remembered Mayor Loretta telling him at the fire victims benefit that her aunt Cathy had practically raised her and she came back here to live with her aunt when she was alone and pregnant with Phoebe. Faith had never mentioned her parents. Hmm. He was curious about Miss Connelly and that was different for him. He didn't ever work up much interest in a woman's life. Faith would tell him that's what a third date was for but that he sent a breakup bouquet instead.

She looked around at her finished work. "What do you think?"

There were flowers everywhere—arrangements of roses—on tables, chairs and the fireplace. The floral scent filled the room and transformed it from an elegant, English-manor ambience to intimate, romantic mountain chateau.

"It looks perfect. You really outdid yourself."

"This is nothing. Wait until you see the room where the reception will be." She smiled up at him. "Let me know what you think when you get home later."

"Wait." He frowned. "Do you have to hurry back for Phoebe?"

"No. She's at a friend's house. Having a sleepover."

"So you'll be here to hear my in-person critique."

She shook her head. "I'm a contractor hired for the job, not a guest at the wedding."

"That's just an oversight." He took out his cell phone and hit speed dial, waiting until it was picked up. "Linc, this is Sam."

"What's up?" His brother sounded in good spirits.

"There's going to be one more at the reception. Is that a problem?"

"No. We planned on that. Why?" There was a slight pause. "You found a plus-one here at the hotel. A snow bunny."

"I hate to break it to you, but it's the end of summer," Sam said wryly. "And no, that's not it. I'm inviting the plant lady. Faith is going to stay."

"I'm sure Rose meant for her to have an invitation. She's had a lot on her mind," Linc said. "But she would love for Faith to be there."

"Okay, it's settled then."

"Good."

"So have you changed your mind about this?" Sam asked, grinning.

"Not a chance. It was my idea and I can't wait." There were voices in the background then Linc said, "I have to go."

The line went dead and Sam grinned. "Can't wait to see how that went."

"I can't stay, Sam. I'm not dressed for it and don't tell me to go change because I don't have any good clothes. They all smell like smoke or are water damaged."

Sam studied her black slacks, cream silk shirt and matching sweater. "You look fine."

"I had to buy a couple of things to get by for working events, but this isn't appropriate for a wedding."

"You look beautiful. And even if you didn't, Linc says you're staying because Rose would love it. And she's the bride. It's her day and she would be disappointed."

Faith pressed her full lips together as she thought about it. "If you're sure."

"I am."

The truth was, *he'd* be disappointed if she wasn't there. For sure he wouldn't be bored now.

A few minutes before five that evening, Faith stood with Sam right outside the banquet room where the wedding ceremony would take place. The double doors were open and guests were arriving.

"I'll just go in by myself and sit in the back," she told him.

"You won't be able to see anything. Trust me, Faith."

"If you say have faith in me, I swear… Everyone else is all dressed up. This is not appropriate."

He grinned and the effect was nuclear. The tuxedo was hard enough for her to deal with. He looked so handsome even *she* wanted to throw her underwear at him. If it was more feminine than the serviceable white cotton she'd bought in desperation from the drug store, she might have considered doing just that. And then he'd smiled and if she'd had the bad judgment to try to speak, gibberish would have been the result.

"Let me tell you something, plant lady, you look beautiful. You're among friends and the bride and groom want you here. If you're still not convinced, we can hang a sign around your neck that says you lost all your stuff in the fire." He took her hand and placed it in the bend of his elbow. "Here we go. I'll take good care of you."

Any further protest flamed out when he touched her. Sam led her to the second row of chairs, directly behind where his family would sit, and directed her to take the seat on the end, to see and hear everything. Since the place was filling up fast and people were looking at her, she did as instructed. Her cheeks felt hot but since everyone was behind her, no one could tell. By the time the row filled in, she was over being embarrassed.

Things started happening fast after that. Sam seated his

mother in the first row. Then a man who looked so much like him it had to be his brother Cal walked a mature woman to the first row across the aisle. That would be Rose's mom, Janie Tucker. When she was settled, he moved to the Hart family side and sat beside his mother.

Finally, Sam took a seat in the first row and Linc stood next to the minister, who was in front of the hearth. He looked so happy she swore there was a collective sigh from every female present. Sam turned to smile at her, and his mother glanced over her shoulder. Oh, boy.

When the traditional wedding march started, the two bridesmaids walked slowly down the aisle. Ellie looked stunning in the off-the-shoulder, lavender-colored dress. The other woman was Ellie's best friend, Vicki Jeffers. Just before the bride appeared, little Leah McKnight marched between the rows of chairs tossing red rose petals on the white runner.

She smiled at Faith. "Hi!"

"Hi," she whispered back.

And then came the main event. Because Faith was on the end she could see the bride walking down the aisle on the arm of a handsome, distinguished older man who bore a strong resemblance to Cal and Sam. That had to be Hastings Hart. So, he was doing double duty as escort and best man.

Rose looked radiant. The sides of her dark hair were pulled back from her face and secured at the crown with three white roses and baby's breath while the rest cascaded down her back. She wore a strapless, floor-length cream silk column dress with a peplum that accentuated her small waist. Her only jewelry was a pair of diamond earrings, stones with some serious carats. She was simple, classic, elegant. A quick glance at the groom's reaction told Faith everything. The man looked as if he'd swallowed his tongue.

When Linc took his bride's hand all he said was, "My beautiful Rose—"

Faith's heart melted. It didn't escape her notice that she wouldn't have been able to see and hear all this if Sam hadn't taken care of her. She looked at him and her heart melted again, for a different reason. In her whole life, the only other person who had ever truly taken care of her was Aunt Cathy.

The wedding party was all in place facing the minister who introduced himself as Reverend Ethan Halstead from the Hart family's church in Dallas. When he asked who gave this woman to this man, Rose's mother proudly answered that she did.

The ceremony wasn't long, but it was solemn, dignified, beautiful, eloquent. Promises of love and fidelity were offered and received, then rings were produced by Hastings Hart. They were exchanged and Rose looked at her diamonds set in platinum band as if she couldn't believe this was really happening.

And then the minister said, "I give you Mr. and Mrs. Lincoln Hart. Take two. You may kiss your bride."

No one had to tell Linc twice and when he dipped Rose back there was loud applause. Faith saw his mother wipe away tears. Then they were surrounded by family and exchanged hugs and handshakes. An announcement was made about the bridal party taking pictures. The guests were instructed to proceed to the reception in the room next door, where a bar was set up and appetizers were being served before dinner.

Faith moved with the crowd. A lot of them were strangers, probably friends from Texas. She waited in line at the bar and ordered a glass of cabernet then circulated among the guests. Here and there she heard comments about how beautiful the flowers were. Because she was anonymous it meant the compliments were sincere. Then the crowd parted and Sam stood in front of her.

"There you are." He had a drink in his hand.

"Hi. I thought you moved heaven and earth to get me here, then you abandoned me." She was only half kidding.

"Would I do that?" He shook his head. "Don't answer that. I want everyone to meet you."

Sam took her hand and led her through the maze of bodies to the bridal table at the front of the room. Ellie looked stunning in her maid of honor dress. Alex was holding Leah, who wasn't letting go of her flower girl basket for anything. They excused themselves to find a snack for their hungry daughter.

A handsome man in his thirties stood a little apart from the tight-knit Harts, looking decidedly ill at ease. And not because of how he was dressed. The dark suit and red silk tie were perfectly tailored to his tall, muscular body.

Because he wasn't in his usual jeans, boots and hat it took Faith a couple beats to recognize the cowboy. "Logan Hunt. It's nice to see you."

"Hi, Faith."

"Obviously you two know each other." Sam sounded a little weird.

"Of course. He has a ranch outside of town." She smiled. "Are you a friend of the bride or groom?"

"Neither." Logan had dark brown hair and intense blue eyes. A lot like all the Harts. "Sam and I are cousins."

"He told me."

The man frowned. "Really? I'm surprised you claimed me, Sam."

Sam met his gaze. "Thanks for coming, Logan. It's good to see you again. I hope we can reconnect"

"Hi, Sam." An older man joined them. "It's been a while."

"Uncle Foster."

Uncle?

The man gave her an appraising look. "Foster Hart. And you are?"

"Faith Connelly." She shook his hand and it wasn't her imagination that he held it longer than necessary. She noticed he also had the Hart eyes, Logan's eyes. This was his father. But something about the man made her uncomfortable.

"Hello, son," Foster said. "Been a long time. How are you?"

"I didn't know he would be here. If someone had clued me in, I wouldn't have come." Logan glared at Sam as if it was his fault.

"Look, Logan, we're family. It's time to put the past behind us and—"

"No." The other man set his untouched drink on the table beside him and walked away.

"All these years and my son hasn't mellowed. He's still as stubborn as when he was a boy." Foster seemed unconcerned. "I think I'll go mingle."

"Well," Faith said, watching until the crowd swallowed him up. "So that's probably a story."

"Yeah. I'll tell you some other time." Sam sighed then slid his arm around her waist. "Come meet the rest of the family."

Walking with him was like being wrapped in a protective shield, a sensation she could get used to if she wasn't careful. For tonight she wasn't going to worry about it. There was a line of Harts and they stopped in front of the tall man at the end of it.

"This is my brother. Cal, meet Faith Connelly."

"Hi." She took the big hand he held out, which was a lot like Sam's, but without the sparks. "Nice to meet you."

"Likewise." His smile was friendly. "In case Sam didn't tell you, I'm the dashing one."

"Says who?" Sam scoffed.

"Me. I pulled out all the stops to get here and rolled in with seconds to spare."

"Don't believe anything he says, Faith. He just likes to make an entrance. Your schedule could benefit from better time management. Just saying..."

"I'm at the whim of renewable energy." Cal shrugged his broad shoulders, perfectly showcased in the expertly tailored tux.

"Where did you fly in from?" she asked.

"Las Vegas. There's a solar energy plant there and I needed to check it out."

"That's exciting." She smiled up at him.

"Yeah, yeah." Sam put his hand to her lower back and urged her forward. "Later, little brother."

"Technically I'm taller, which makes you the little brother," Cal said behind her.

"Don't pay any attention to him. Faith, this is my mother, Katherine Hart, and my father, Hastings."

"It's a pleasure to meet you both." What a striking, attractive couple, she thought. The man was tall, like his sons, with a full head of silver hair. His mother's was stylishly cut into a bob and probably colored. As beautiful as she still was, this woman had probably been stunning when she was younger. Faith had a sudden case of nerves. "I'm so sorry I'm not dressed appropriately—"

"You look beautiful," Katherine said. "You're the young woman Sam took in because of the fire."

"Yes. Me and my daughter."

"She lost a lot of personal belongings," Sam explained. "And Faith is the plant lady."

"Hastings, she did these exquisite flowers. And the beautiful arrangement Sam had sent for my birthday."

"You're very talented." Hastings looked impressed.

"I learned from the best. My aunt Cathy taught me

everything. When she passed away, she left me the business she'd built. Every Bloomin' Thing."

"Clever name," Katherine said approvingly.

"She was a clever lady." As well as kind and patient. More than just arranging flowers, her aunt had taught her about maternal love.

"And Rose's bouquet," the woman said. "It's so lovely. Those roses are simply stunning."

"The color symbolizes everlasting love," Sam said. "And the lavender bridesmaids' flowers signify love at first sight."

"And how do you know that?" his father asked.

"Faith told me."

There was so much she could say now about his flower choices, but Faith had just met his parents. When she kept her mouth shut, he gave her a grateful look.

Katherine pointed to the activity in the center of the room where the crowd was backing up. "I think Rose is getting ready to toss that stunning bouquet. She said she wanted to get this done before dinner so she could relax."

Hastings nodded. "They're calling for all the single women. Faith, you're not married, are you?"

"No, but—"

"Then you best get out there, young lady."

Hastings Hart wasn't the sort of man one said no to. The only thing that made her feel better was that right after the bouquet, it was time to throw the garter. Faith joined the group and stood close to the front, guessing Rose would give it a pretty solid over-the-shoulder throw to someone near the back. That's exactly what happened and when she met Sam's gaze, she shrugged.

Then it was time for the guys and there were a lot of whistles and good-natured teasing when they gathered. Sam neatly avoided the lacy thing Linc shot over his shoulder like a rubber band. And he shrugged at her.

He moved to her side and looked down. "I guess you're empty-handed and will be a spinster forever."

"Back at you. Say what you want, but I'm relieved. There's no pressure to be the next one to get married."

"Hail to the bachelor," he said in solidarity.

"I'm glad that's over."

"Amen."

"Now we can enjoy the festivities," she said. "And by that I mean food. I worked through lunch to get the flowers done. I'm starving."

"Yeah, me too— Damn it." He was looking over her shoulder at someone.

She turned to see Linc motioning him over. "It would appear that you're being paged."

"Whatever it is, I'll make it quick." He met her gaze.

"Famous last words," she scoffed.

"Promise me a dance?" he challenged.

"A waste of breath since you're going to abandon me."

"Oh, ye of little faith."

He went off to do his thing after giving her a smile that promised something more than just his company at the reception. Her toes curled, her knees went weak and she was counting the seconds until she could find out what more he had in mind.

Chapter Ten

Sam's family obligations at the reception turned out to be more extensive than he'd anticipated. Finally dinner was served, toasts made and his responsibilities complete. It was time to collect that dance from Faith. He searched the room and finally saw her sitting at a table not far from the door. She had her cell phone in her hand and, if body language was anything to go by, looked ready to make a quick escape.

It was now or never and he had some figurative dancing to do in order to distract her from the fact that he'd abandoned her as she'd predicted. Due to family commitments, but still…

He crossed the room and stopped beside her table, holding out his hand. "They're playing our song."

"Does that cheesy line ever work for you?"

"There's always a first time. You promised me a dance."

"Not exactly," she reminded him. "I said it was a waste of breath because you were going to abandon me. And I was right."

"Blame the bridal couple. They've got this thing for pictures to commemorate this day and for some reason my presence in them was mandatory."

Surprisingly, her face softened. "You're fortunate to have people who want you in their life and memories."

"Does that mean you'll dance with me?"

"It does." She put her fingers in the hand he was still holding out and let him pull her to her feet.

Right there by the table he settled her close and started moving to the slow song. If she wondered why he couldn't wait to get her to the center of the room where other couples were dancing, she didn't ask. And he didn't want her to think about it. The lights were low, the mood was intimate. That was good enough for him. She felt nice in his arms and he sighed, as if he'd been holding his breath for a very long time in anticipation of this exact moment.

"Are you sorry you stayed for all this?" he asked.

"No." She slid her hand farther over his shoulder. "Are you sorry you got me an invitation to crash the party?"

"Only a little."

"Really?" She leaned back far enough to look at him.

"I was sorry you had to see that scene with my cousin Logan." Their feet were barely moving. This conversation could have happened sitting at the table but the slow song gave him a chance to keep holding her. "He has issues with his father."

"He's not a dedicated flower consumer like yourself, so I don't know him well." She grinned at her not-so-subtle reference to his dating history. "But the tension between the two of them was obvious. I haven't heard anything bad about Logan. And in this town, I would have. Especially the bad stuff. It spreads faster than the flu."

"He is a good guy, no thanks to his father. My uncle is—" Sam tried to think how to diplomatically label the underhanded, integrity-challenged, womanizing bastard.

"Let's just say he's the polar opposite of his brother. My father."

"Hastings Hart sets a high bar."

Sam brushed his thumb lightly over her back and wished he could feel her bare skin. "Oh?"

"Your father knew Linc wasn't his son, but he accepted the child as his own and no one was the wiser. Not just any man could pull it off."

"True." Sam nodded. "I don't know whether or not that makes him a good man. Just one who would do anything for the woman he loves."

"Hmm."

"What does that mean?" Another song started to play and Sam's luck held when the slow, sweet strains of a ballad filled the room.

"I was just thinking about Linc and Rose. They were split up for ten years and it was finalizing their divorce that brought them back together."

"Because they never got over each other. And they're still madly in love."

She shrugged. "They got lucky."

"That's one way of putting it," he said drily.

"You know that's not what I meant." She playfully punched his shoulder. "Let me rephrase. They are among the fortunate few who found their soul mate."

"And came close to losing each other. Who knew a lawyer would be responsible for bringing two people back together?"

"I know what you mean." She laughed. "For the record, romantic attorney is sort of an oxymoron."

"You got the 'moron' part right. If Linc had hired a barracuda like my ex-wife did..."

"Or like my ex-husband."

The light was too dim to really see her face, but he didn't hear anger or bitterness in her voice. He wanted to know what was going through her mind and if she didn't want to answer, she would tell him. So he asked, "What are you thinking?"

"Love complicates everything. Things would have been fine if he and I hadn't taken that step."

"You mean marriage," he said.

"No, way before that. If we'd just stayed friends. Friendship is so much better."

He thought back, to the beginning of his relationship with the woman he'd married. She was funny and beautiful. There had been hints that she was mercenary, spiteful and self-centered, but he'd ignored them. He'd been in a hurry to leap into love and if he hadn't been, things might have been different.

"You know," he said, "now that I think about it, friendship *is* better. Do you have a flower for that?"

"A forever friendship flower?" She looked thoughtful. "I'd have to do some research. Off the top of my head, I would make it a daisy. They're pleasant and cheerful. Who doesn't like daisies?"

"That would be like despising kittens, puppies and butterflies." The music stopped but he didn't let her go.

"Did I just come up with your new dating strategy? Is there something you want to tell me?"

"Yes. I really—" A fast song blared from the speakers and seemed to vibrate the whole room. It didn't do his hearing any favors, either.

"What did you say?" Faith shouted.

Sam saw a lot of people flood the dance floor and knew the DJ was trying to shake things up. That didn't work for his purposes. "I said, I really li—"

She shook her head. "Can't hear you."

Sam grabbed her hand and tugged her through the doors and into the hall, which was also vibrating. The wall didn't stop the harsh sounds. Looking around he saw an exit sign. Without letting go of Faith, he walked toward it and didn't stop until they were standing outside on the hotel's patio. The air was cool and smelled of pine and flowers. There was a shrub-lined sidewalk with benches, chairs and old-fashioned streetlights. A nearly full moon hung in the spectacular sky and, most of all, it was quiet. If there was also an element of romance, well, he would just count his lucky stars.

"Oh, thank God." Faith took a deep breath and let it out.

Sam was mesmerized by the simple movement of her chest. Moments ago it was pressed against him and he missed the feel of her.

"Sam?"

"Hmm?" He lifted his gaze to hers.

"What were you trying to say in there? Before the music broke my ears."

He couldn't remember. Apparently he was *that* guy and easily distracted by a woman's assets. More likely it was specifically about Faith. "What were we talking about?"

"Friendship. Leaving love out of it."

"Right." Now he remembered. "Relationships as defined by Faith Connelly."

"You think I'm wrong?"

"On the contrary, I completely concur."

"You do?" She blinked up at him. "When did the sun, moon and stars align so that we're in agreement about something? I must have missed that."

"Smart aleck." The fact that she could make him smile was one of his favorite things about her. "I like you, Faith. That's what I was saying in there."

Her face softened. "I like you, too."

"And I like Phoebe. She's smart and funny. Really terrific. If I could pick any kid in the world it would be her."

"Aww." She smiled as if he'd handed her a star. "And

that just proves that there's hope for you. In terms of your judgment about women."

"I'm serious. Your friendship means a lot to me and I don't want to lose it. But—"

She pressed a finger to his mouth to stop the next words. "That's not going to happen to us."

He thought about it for a moment and nodded. "On the plus side, we have been living under the same roof for a while now and we still enjoy each other's company."

"See?" She tilted her head to look up at him. "That's because we haven't complicated it with sex."

The pathway lights illuminated her expression and Sam saw the exact second when teasing turned to awareness. Suddenly her eyes were wide and her lips parted slightly.

His serial dating days had taught him something about women. He knew when one was feeling sexual tension and he could see it crackling in Faith right now. If that wasn't enough, her breathing was shallow and fast.

He cupped her face in his hands and lowered his mouth to hers. The touch was meant to be sweet and tender but quickly turned hot and demanding. He traced her lips with his tongue and she opened to him, letting him invade and explore. She settled her hands on his chest, pressing closer, and he slid an arm around her waist, holding her tighter.

The sound of their harsh breathing filled his ears, drowning out the night sounds. He wanted her and she wanted him right back. *But*... There was that damn word again.

He lifted his head, leaving only millimeters between their mouths. "Faith, I wish we— But we can't— There's a—"

"Wedding reception," she said, her voice barely a whisper.

"Yeah." He stepped away from temptation and willed her to believe what he was going to say. "You should know this isn't sudden, kissing you, I mean."

"I know. It wasn't for me, either."

"I've wanted to do that for a while."

"I can't say I haven't wanted you to."

"Okay, then—" He blew out a long breath. "Fair warning. At an appropriate time, there will be more kissing. And stuff—unless you're not interested. I'll back off. No harm, no foul. Just say the word and—"

She shook her head. "I'm all in favor of—stuff."

"Good."

"It's love I have a problem with."

So did he. How perfect was that?

The afternoon following the wedding, Faith had picked Phoebe up at her friend's house and was headed back to Sam's. Her daughter's sleepovers rarely resulted in a lot of sleep so she was normally quiet afterward and today was no exception.

Having time to mull over what had happened with Sam the night before at the reception may, or may not, have been a good thing. But unless aliens landed their spaceship in front of her van, forcing her thoughts in a different direction, she was compelled to think about kissing him. There was debatable satisfaction in the fact that she'd been right. He made a move and she hadn't pushed him away. What's more, she'd basically given him a rain check for sex.

Those persistent tingles of hers kicked into high gear at the anticipation she'd seen in his eyes. Since Phoebe was at her friend's, they probably would have continued their make-out session at the house, but Sam had brought Cal home with him. His brother's visit had been so last-minute he had nowhere to stay. So that was that.

She pulled into the driveway and it was hard to miss a couple of cars parked in front that hadn't been there when she left. "Hmm."

"Who's here?" Phoebe asked.

"That's an excellent question. I have no idea."

She found an unoccupied space for her van and the two of them went inside. Phoebe set her backpack at the bottom of the stairs and they followed the loud sound of voices that led them to the kitchen. No one noticed them standing in the doorway, what with most of the Hart family gathered there. Hastings, Katherine, Cal and Alex McKnight stood around the island. It was a good bet Ellie and Leah were around somewhere.

Faith had the random thought that these men could easily be Mr. September, October, November and December on a hunky guy calendar.

"Mom?" Phoebe saw the strangers and moved closer.

Sam must have heard because he looked over and smiled. "Hey, Squirt. How was the sleepover?"

"Good." She put her hand in Faith's.

"Don't be afraid, Phoebs. This is my family. Although I know they look like it, no one is a fugitive from an asylum." Sam slapped his brother on the back. "Except maybe Cal here."

"Cal was raised by wolves and left on my doorstep when they didn't want him anymore." Hastings walked over and held out his hand to the little girl. "I'm Sam's dad. You must be Phoebe. I met your mom yesterday and I've heard a lot about you."

"Really?" She put her little hand in his bigger one.

"Yes." He winked. "Sam tells me you're a troublemaker."

"No, he didn't," the little girl loyally defended.

"You're right. He didn't." The older man gently took her by the hand. "Let me introduce you to everyone. Except Linc and Rose, who are on their honeymoon. This is Sam's brother, Calhoun, and his mother, who is also my wife, Katherine. She's much nicer than I am."

"You're pretty nice," Phoebe said. "Like Sam."

Hastings smiled fondly. "He gets that from me."

Faith was swept into the chaos and ended up sitting at the table in the nook with Katherine Hart. Phoebe was looking at ease with the hunky Hart men but Faith had a sudden case of nerves because she really cared about making a good impression. Not that she wanted Sam's mom to hate her, but it shouldn't be this big a deal what the woman thought of her. Except it *was* a big deal and that was a troubling sign.

"It's nice to see you again, Mrs. Hart."

"Katherine, please." She smiled. "I'm so pleased you were able to join us at the reception yesterday. And it has to be said again how perfect the flowers were. Rose was so happy with everything and that made my son happy, too."

"I'm glad. Thank you for telling me. And for including me in the festivities."

"Technically Rose and Linc hosted, but I know they were glad you were there."

"Yes, they told me." She clenched her hands in her lap, beneath the table, so tight her fingers started to lose sensation. "The truth is that Sam insisted. He wouldn't take no for an answer."

"Is that so?"

Faith hadn't meant to blurt that out but she was stuck now. "Not even the fact that I wasn't properly dressed for the occasion could sway him."

"He's stubborn. Always was. He was determined to marry that society schemer." A shadow crossed her face when she looked at him across the room, laughing with the men. Then she seemed to shake it off. "Sorry."

"No problem. He told me about the divorce."

"Funny," she said. "Divorce was a game changer for both of my sons—one in a bad way, the other good. It scarred Sam and brought Linc and Rose back together."

Faith had no idea what to say to that. So a change of subject was in order. "Where's Ellie?"

"Potty training," Katherine answered.

"I'm going to assume you mean Leah," Faith teased. "Probably Ellie is competent in that regard."

"Yes." Katherine laughed. "I promise not to boast that she came out of the womb proficient in all things potty."

"Bless you for not being one of those mothers whose little darling was trained by his or her first birthday."

"Heaven forbid. That drove me crazy," the older woman admitted. "I felt like a failure as a mother if mine weren't taking care of business by themselves when the so-called pediatric experts said they should be."

"I know, right?" Faith realized the nerves were gone because this woman was down-to-earth and real, not pretending to be a superwoman.

"Mom, are you telling secrets about me?" Sam wandered over and put his hand on her shoulder.

"Of course." Katherine gave him a sassy look. "A mother knows where all the bodies are buried."

"Just kill me now." He looked heavenward and sighed. "And the day started out so promising. Then Ellie declared my house was a family dinner zone. Without my knowledge or consent, I might add."

"Stop whining," his mother teased. "We brought all the food. You're just providing the party house."

"And I felt so special. Right up until the zinger." He looked at Faith and there was a gleam in his eyes. "So much for a quiet Sunday."

"Peace and tranquility are highly overrated," she said. Especially when there was very little tranquility and not a lot of peace because all she could think about was the next time she could kiss Sam—alone. Except aliens, in the guise of his relatives, had landed and she was forced to put personal stuff on a back burner where it would simmer slowly.

"Bebe!" Leah ran into the room and threw her arms

around Phoebe, then said at the top of her lungs, "You here. I big girl. Go pee pee in the potty!"

"She's such a delicate flower." Ellie sighed and sat down beside Faith at the table. "I don't think they heard her in Cleveland."

"It will get better," Faith and Katherine said together.

"Great minds." The older woman held up her hand for a high five.

"Bebe," Leah said even louder, in case her mother was right about Cleveland, "wanna go in Unca Sam's pool?"

"Along with an outstanding pair of lungs," Ellie said, "she just had a really good idea. Listen up, guys, last one in the pool is a rotten egg!"

And the pitch of Ellie's voice was proof that the apple did not fall far from the tree, Faith thought. It did, however, produce results. Thirty minutes later, Phoebe and Leah were in the water with Sam, Cal and Alex. The grandparents were stretched out on lounges under an umbrella and snapping cell phone photos of the swimmers as well as selfies. Faith and Ellie sat at the patio table in the shade with tall glasses of iced tea in front of them.

"I hope you don't mind that we all descended on you without warning," Ellie said.

"Of course not. My daughter is having a blast, which means I can relax. You brought food and you're fun—" Faith stopped. That sounded as if she belonged here and that so wasn't the case. This was Sam's house and she was only temporary. "It's your brother's call."

Ellie nodded. "I thought a mini family reunion, minus the honeymooners, would be nice because it's not often we get Cal here." She glanced at the pool where the men were playing a spirited game of Marco Polo with the little girls. "Sam didn't take the really broad hints I was dropping about a gathering. Then Cal announced he was bunking here since Mom and Dad are at my house and he needed somewhere to stay. Sam looked ready to strangle him, which I don't get."

Faith did. Like her, he'd thought they would be alone to pick up where they'd left off. She was both relieved and disappointed when it didn't happen. Her skin felt too tight and there was a knot of tension inside her, just waiting to be tapped. She hadn't been with a man in a very long time and had forgotten how good it felt to be held and kissed and wanted. Then Sam had unleashed it all under the moon and stars last night. It just had to be acknowledged that he had some serious skills when it came to kissing.

She'd been anticipating exploring the rest of his skill set because there'd been no doubt they'd end up in his bed. Then fate had intervened. That gave her a chance to wonder whether or not it would be a mistake to upset the way things were.

"Maggie Potter told me yesterday how much she loved the wedding flowers. She's going to make an appointment to talk to you about doing them for her wedding to Sloan Holden."

"I'm glad to hear that. It seems weddings in this town are contagious. Not that I'm complaining, because it's great for my business. It's just—" She glanced at Sam, who was letting Phoebe splash him without retaliation. He'd wanted kids once, before the social schemer tried to take him for everything.

"What?" Ellie prodded.

"You and Alex are happy, right?" As soon as the words were out of her mouth she was horrified. "I'm sorry. That was rude and an invasion of your privacy. Not to mention none of my business."

"Don't be silly. There's nothing I would rather talk about than Alex and me. We're very happy and deliriously in love."

"And Leah is—" She didn't know how to phrase the

question. Was she an intruder in their love? Did they resent her for being there? Or tune her out in their devotion to each other?

"I was pregnant with Leah when we married," Ellie said. "But she's the best thing that ever happened to both of us. She completes our family. Until another baby comes along."

"You want more?"

"Oh, yes. Don't tell anyone, but we're trying to get pregnant." The other woman glowed. "Alex and I didn't have to get married because of the pregnancy. We did it because we love each other."

"How do you know it will last?"

"There are no guarantees. But if you find a good man who makes your heart beat as if it will jump out of your chest and you count the seconds until he comes home, those are pretty good signs that you're in love for the long haul."

That pretty well described how she felt about Sam. It would be so much easier if she didn't, because their friendship was working and had become important to her. As much as she wanted him, taking the next step could ruin the best relationship she'd ever had.

Damn this annoying attraction.

Chapter Eleven

"So, how does your day look?"

Sam sat across the table from Faith. Eating breakfast with her and Phoebe was becoming one of the bright spots in his day. The two of them collaborated on cooking scrambled eggs, toast and fruit. Phoebe was noisily slurping cereal.

"I've got a busy one," she answered. "Filling and delivering orders. Sunday your sister told me that Maggie Potter really liked the flowers at the wedding and was going to call me for a consultation. There was a message waiting when I walked in the door yesterday."

He sipped his coffee and savored the rich flavor that tasted so much better when Faith made it. "What's so important that she had to call bright and early on Monday morning?"

"Her wedding."

"Is it just me," he asked, "or are weddings in this town becoming an epidemic?"

"I said something along those lines to Ellie when she

mentioned it the other day. But one shouldn't complain about good fortune. I'm going to need the money to fix my house."

"How's that coming?"

"Alex has a crew ready to start as soon as the building inspector clears it, hopefully at the end of the week. First we need to see what can be salvaged, then demolition is the next step."

"Good." That was an automatic response. The tightening in his gut when the meaning of her words sank in was not. It was becoming clear to him that all the bright spots in his day included Faith. There was a clock ticking on these breakfasts with her and he wasn't ready for them to end when she moved out.

"That reminds me, Sam. My meeting with Maggie might run late. I hate to ask—"

"I'll pick Phoebe up from camp."

"I don't need to be picked up." The camper in question pushed away her bowl with the cereal gone and milk remaining. "I'm going home with Melissa. You said I could sleep over, remember? Because summer's almost over."

"I do now," Faith answered. "Problem solved."

Was it? Sam wondered. Or did that just create a different one? Her cheeks turned pink and she wouldn't quite meet his gaze, telling him she realized the two of them would be all alone in the house. The last time they were alone, he kissed her and she kissed him back before admitting she was interested in more. Had she changed her mind?

Before he could figure out how to ask in a way an eight-year-old wouldn't pick up on, the doorbell rang. He met her gaze. "Are you expecting anyone?"

"No. You?"

Sam shook his head and got up. "I'll see who it is."

"We have to get going." Faith stood, reaching for his plate.

"I'll clear." He touched her hand and she looked at him.

There were sparks in her eyes and her breath caught. A good sign that she hadn't changed her mind. The bell sounded again. "But first I'll answer the door."

"Get your things, Phoebe. The bus is leaving." She walked out of the room.

Sam headed for the entryway and opened the front door. His mother stood there. "Mom. Hi."

"Good morning." As always she looked beautiful, in her royal blue silky slacks and matching top. "May I come in?"

"Sure." He stepped back and pulled the door wide.

She kissed his cheek, then said, "I hope I'm not interrupting anything."

Faith walked in with Phoebe behind her. "Hi, Katherine. We were just leaving. I have to get my darling daughter to camp then open the shop."

"Then my timing is perfect," she said. "I just wanted to stop in and say goodbye. Hastings and I are flying back to Dallas this morning."

"Do you hafta go?" Phoebe said, genuine disappointment in her voice.

"I'm afraid so, sweetie." Katherine smiled regretfully. "I have commitments at home. The annual fund-raiser for the children's hospital is coming up and I'm the chairwoman."

"I'm going to miss you." The little girl looked a little mopey.

"You are so adorable." Spontaneously Katherine leaned down to hug the child. "Now tell me the truth. It's because you're going to miss beating me at checkers, isn't it?"

"That, too." Phoebe grinned and there was mischief written all over it.

"I'll be back soon for a rematch, sweetheart."

"Better be soon," the little girl said. "When our house is fixed we won't be here anymore."

"Have no fear. We'll work something out." Katherine looked at Faith. "I've enjoyed getting to know you."

"I feel the same about you." She glanced up at Sam. "You raised a good man. One who would take in people with nowhere else to go."

"He is a good man." His mother's look was full of approval and pride and something else that was the reason for this visit. "I hope we'll see you the next time we're in Blackwater Lake. We try to make the trip often to see our little Leah."

"I look forward to it." Faith put her hand on Phoebe's shoulder. "Sorry, I really have to run."

"Of course. Don't let me keep you."

Sam watched her get the little girl into the van then climb into the driver's side. He didn't close the door until her vehicle disappeared from sight, then he looked at his mother. "Coffee?"

"No offense, dear, but yours is dreadful."

"Faith made it."

"Then yes." She smiled. "I'd love some. If you're not in a hurry to get to the office."

"No."

"Okay, then." She followed him into the kitchen, where he grabbed a mug and poured the dark, hot liquid into it. "Here you go."

"Thank you."

Sam moved to the table and stacked the breakfast plates. "To what do I owe this visit?"

"I just wanted to see you one more time before we leave." She sat at the kitchen table and wrapped her hands around the cup with steam rising from it. "I really like your Faith."

And there was the ulterior motive. "She's not mine."

Although she might be later that night. Anticipation rolled through him. "I'm just being a good neighbor to her and her daughter. Extending a helping hand."

"Is that what you young people call it these days?" There was a twinkle in her eyes.

"Why, whatever do you mean?"

"I raised you to be a good man, not a dense one." Her expression said *duh*. "You know very well I'm talking about sex."

Sam cringed and was pretty sure it showed. He couldn't count high enough to enumerate the number of reasons he did not want to discuss this with his mother. "No, no, no. I call time-out."

"Gotcha." His mother grinned. "It's so easy, Sam."

"Then I have it on the record that you're not above deliberately torturing your children?"

"If anyone asks I'll deny it. But I couldn't resist. And, really, you and Faith looked so close."

"And I suppose that means that you're not going to leave it at 'gotcha'?"

"Not a chance," she said.

"Okay." He let out a long-suffering sigh. "I'm not sleeping with her."

"Yet," his mother said.

How did she do that? he wondered. How did she know he'd been thinking about it? This was creepy. Sometimes it was best to say nothing and this was one of those times.

"Sam, it was nice seeing you with Faith. And Phoebe..." Katherine smiled fondly. "She's a wonderful little girl and you're so good with her. Clearly she adores you."

"What can I say? The kid has good taste."

"I'm your mother. You'll get no argument from me. But it made me hopeful watching you with them."

He was going to be sorry, but couldn't help himself. "Hopeful of what?"

"That you'll settle down and have a family of your own. I worry about that."

"Don't," he urged.

"Telling a mother not to worry is like ordering rain not to fall." She met his gaze and there was concern in hers. "It's wonderful to see you so happy. Everyone says you and Faith are perfect for each other."

"First of all, there's no such thing as perfect. And second, who's everyone?"

"Ellie."

"A consensus of one," he said triumphantly. "That doesn't make it true."

"Doesn't make it not true, either." Her tone changed to the one she used when going in for the kill. "Look at it this way. You're not getting any younger. If you're going to give me grandchildren, you better get busy."

"At the risk of pointing out the obvious, you already have a beautiful granddaughter, Mom."

"I want, and frankly I'm expecting, all of my children to reproduce."

"You might have to lower your expectations."

"That's not going to happen." Katherine had on her "because I'm the mom" face. "Grandchildren are a parent's reward for not strangling their teenagers."

"Hey, I wasn't that bad," he protested.

"You weren't there."

He grinned. "Technically, I was."

"Not as a parent. You haven't walked in those shoes. Talk to me again after you do."

"Not likely." Having kids without tying the knot wasn't an option for him and he didn't believe in marriage anymore. "Not for me."

Katherine sighed. "I know you're worried about making another mistake, Sam, but Faith is not that woman."

"That's for sure." Karen Leigh Perry was in a class by herself. Just thinking her name brought back the bitterness that showed no signs of ever fading.

"For the sake of argument, let me just say that a good

marriage is worth all the trouble and no one knows that better than I do."

Wow, she was hinting at the cracks in her relationship with his father. This was a first, and he was really surprised. "I've never heard you talk about that."

"Maybe I should have." There were shadows in his mother's eyes. "It might have been a mistake to sweep it under the rug and present a picture-perfect front. That was a difficult time and both your father and I wanted to forget about what happened. But now I believe it might have been a disservice to you. You're the oldest and the one who remembers the most, and were probably affected by it more than your brother. I'm concerned that my silence contributed to your fear of commitment."

"I'm not afraid of committing." That was knee-jerk and so macho. No guy would admit to being afraid of anything.

"That's a discussion to be taken up at a later time. For purposes of this conversation I just want to say marriage isn't easy. Your father and I are proof of that. But we love each other very much and were willing to do the work. We came back from the brink and..." She smiled. "It's magic. I can't imagine my life without him. Being together, with a man who supports me unconditionally and loves me in spite of my flaws. Having coffee in the morning and talking about our plans for the day."

Not unlike what he'd just experienced with Faith. Woo woo weird. "I appreciate you telling me this, Mom."

"You're welcome." The cell phone in her purse signaled and she looked at it. "It's a text from your father. The plane is just about ready."

"Okay."

"Your face gives nothing away," Katherine said, "but inside you're doing the dance of joy because I have to be finished talking about this, aren't you?"

"I neither confirm nor deny."

She stood and put her hand on his cheek. "Do me a favor and wait until I leave to celebrate."

"I won't be celebrating. Believe it or not, I appreciate what you just told me." He kissed her cheek. "And I'll miss beating you at checkers, too."

"Brat."

"That's me."

"I love you, Sam."

"Back at you." He walked her to the car and watched until she was gone.

Sam was still getting over his shock that his mother even brought up that dark time when she and his father nearly divorced. Then he thought about Faith. Her sassy sense of humor and sexy mouth. He had to admit that the idea of being more than friends with her didn't make him sweat. Was it because she was dead set against love, making her different from most women? But what if he and Faith were perfect together? That was an intriguing thought.

As she'd expected, Faith was late getting back to Sam's after work. She'd come up with flower ideas that Maggie loved, but it had taken time. Sam was in the kitchen when she arrived and she joined him there. Just as she walked in her cell phone signaled a text message. It was from Phoebe's friend's mom.

Got Phoebe. We're home. Girls are having a blast. Will take them to camp in the a.m.

Faith set her purse on one of the bar stools at the kitchen island and texted back.

Thanx. I owe you. When my house is fixed, it's my turn.

Almost immediately there was a happy face emoji, indicating the message was received.

"Everything okay?" Sam asked, standing with the island between them.

"Fine. Phoebe is safe and sound."

"Excellent. Would you like a glass of wine?"

"It's like you can read my mind."

"If only..." He grinned. "Have a seat."

She didn't need an invitation, what with her knees going all weak and wobbly. He should have a warning label for that smile that said: "Beware, prolonged exposure could result in acute light-headedness." Then it hit her that she wasn't really a guest or one of his women. She was displaced and he was doing her a favor. She should be earning her keep.

Instantly she stood and walked around the island. "You don't need to be waiting on me. Why don't I cook dinner?"

He handed her the glass of chardonnay he'd just poured. "Because it's already cooked."

"Funny." She glanced around at the spotless stove. "There's not a dirty pot or pan in sight. Did you wiggle your nose and make a magical meal? Invisible meat loaf? No calories so it doesn't go to your hips?"

Holding a beer, he stood there in his snug, worn jeans and the sleeves of his white shirt were rolled up to mid-forearm. "Except for the calorie part, I'm almost that good."

She would bet on it and wasn't thinking food. The idea made her heart race. "Don't keep me in suspense."

"On the way home I made a stop at the Harvest Café and got takeout."

She smiled. "You win."

"That could be jumping the gun. You might want to wait until I reveal the menu. Hint—it's not meatloaf."

"I don't even care," she said. "Lucy Bishop is a genius

with food and, as long as I didn't have to be involved, you are king of the kitchen."

"If only I could claim that title, but my motives were completely self-serving. It was all about me." He shrugged. "No time for lunch. Which is why I also got dessert. If you haven't had Lucy Bishop's decadent chocolate cake, you're in for a real treat."

"You must be starving. You didn't have to wait for me," she protested.

"I know."

Reading between the lines, she had to conclude he *wanted* to wait. Oh, boy, that could turn a girl's head. "Then let's get you fed, mister."

In ten minutes they were sitting at the table in the nook sharing a bottle of wine while eating salad and shrimp risotto. It was almost like a date. And that made her realize something. "You're not going out."

Sam finished chewing the last of his salad. "What?"

"It just occurred to me that you aren't seeing women."

His eyes crinkled at the corners as he smiled. "Unless there's something you want to tell me, I'm pretty sure I'm seeing one right now."

"You're deliberately misunderstanding me."

"How do you know I haven't gone out with someone?"

She could cite the most obvious indicator: he was home every night. Except Faith was afraid to go with that because it was too domestic—a sign that he was a family man. Although that wasn't experience talking since she didn't have any clue what a normal family looked like. The idea of it pushed her buttons, all the dangerous ones that made her ache to know what it felt like.

"You haven't bought any first-date flowers," she finally said. "And don't think I haven't noticed the drop in my revenue."

"If Phoebe's college fund is a little thin, I'll make a generous contribution," he said wryly.

"It will be an investment in America's youth." She took a sip of wine. "But seriously, I hope that you taking us in hasn't cramped your style. If so, we can find somewhere else to go until the house repairs are finished."

"Jumping to conclusions isn't the best way to burn calories," he teased.

"I'm not joking, Sam. I would really like to know if we're putting you out."

"I would tell you." He took a bite of shrimp and chewed thoughtfully. "For that matter, you'd know if I had a problem with our living arrangement."

"So you don't? All cards on the table," she said.

"Honestly, I've enjoyed having you here. Both of you," he added. "That child of yours is terrific. I really get a kick out of her."

She could tell he cared about Phoebe just by the amount of time he spent with her and the little girl was eating it up. Faith's father had interacted with her very little, and she was completely invisible to him when her mother was around. She didn't know how it felt to be daddy's little girl or have her father wrapped around her little finger.

"Faith?"

"Hmm?"

"You have a funny look on your face."

"Do I?" The memories weren't funny at all. They were profoundly lonely and sad. "Sorry. You were saying?"

"Just—don't worry about moving out, okay?"

She nodded, then made a serious dent in the food on her plate, studying him at the same time. Apparently she was feeling the urge to be bold tonight because she said, "Now you have a funny look on your face. Care to talk about why?"

He seemed to wrestle with whether or not to tell her,

then seemed to make a decision. "My mom said something this morning, before she left."

"Oh?"

"For the first time ever she talked about when she and my dad were separated. It's noteworthy because when they got back together and she was pregnant with Linc the subject never came up. Even when we got older and had relationship issues of our own, there was no mention of it."

"What did she say today?"

"That marriage isn't easy but if you're willing to do the work it can be magic."

"Isn't that kind of a no-brainer? No offense to your mom."

"The thing is, she thinks never bringing it up could be responsible for the fact that I haven't gotten serious about a woman since my divorce."

"Is she right?"

"No." He finished off his wine then refilled her glass from the bottle before pouring more into his. "I can't deny that I'd like to settle down, but the fact is that I haven't found anyone I like."

"Kiki didn't do it for you?"

"I like you." He laughed. "If I met someone like you, the thought of marriage wouldn't make me hyperventilate. Because you're funny, smart, pretty and a good mom."

He thought she was pretty? Way to bury the lede, she thought. But she was liking this. "Go on."

"If we were married I could get a break on buying flowers."

"If we were married there wouldn't be any more first dates so that would save you a bundle of money right there. Just saying," she told him.

"Smart aleck. The truth is, I believe you're honest and honorable."

By "honorable" she knew he meant she wasn't the type to make his life a living hell if they split. This was turning out to be an interesting conversation. She was sure he was only talking so candidly because he'd made it clear to Faith that no woman could make him want to get married again. She would go along, play "what if."

"My turn." She sipped her wine then said, "From my perspective, your pro-marriage bullet points are as follows—good sense of humor, which means you're smart. Funny people are. You're not hard on the eyes. And you're a good, decent man. Responsible. On top of that you could fund Phoebe's college education with one hand tied behind your back. I've already said I think you'd be a great dad. Phoebe could do worse. Oh, and she really likes you, too."

"So what we have here is mutual like for each other." He held up his wineglass. "What should we drink to?"

Faith thought for a moment then touched her glass to his. "Here's to you not putting love on the list."

He didn't drink to that. "What is it about love that bothers you so much?"

"You mean other than the fact that my ex clearly wasn't feeling it for me?"

"Yes," he said. "Even after a bad relationship most people, in time, are willing to try again."

"You're not," she pointed out.

"That's about the legalities of it, not the emotions." He frowned. "But there's something going on with you. A core belief that shapes your views."

How very perceptive of him. Faith realized she might have underestimated his depth. Maybe it was the wine, or just the fact that she needed to get it off her chest, but the words came pouring out. "I don't think I ever told you why my aunt Cathy left her business to me."

"I just figured she didn't have children."

"Yes, but it's more than that. I was the child she never had and she was the parent I didn't have." She swirled the contents of her glass. "My mother and father are gone now.

In fact they died less than a year apart, but I was an adult by then. They were extremely close. Even worked together at their travel agency business in Helena. They traveled a lot, seeing the world together. Just the two of them. At some point they just left me with my aunt because I was there most of the time anyway. The two of them were completely wrapped up in each other. The only explanation I ever got for them ignoring me was that they were madly in love and it was too consuming to let anyone else in."

Sam stared at her for several moments. "So the message you got is that love is exclusionary?"

"Yes." She shrugged. "And now I have Phoebe and I love her with all my heart. I can't take the chance that my feelings for a man would leave her out."

"It doesn't have to," he said rationally.

"Intellectually, I know you're right, but I have no proof of that. I won't risk her happiness."

"Of all the irresponsible, selfish behavior— Your parents, not you." The muscle in Sam's jaw clenched as he gritted his teeth.

Faith had never seen him look like that, so angry he might snap the stem of the glass in his hand. "I'm over it."

"The hell you are." His voice was a growl. "But now I understand. Your childhood left a bigger scar than your husband did."

"Well, it is what it is." She wanted to tease the fury from his expression. "And based on our tragic pasts, we are, hypothetically speaking, well-suited to each other."

"For all the reasons we just listed," he agreed.

"Exactly. Except there's one thing we didn't mention." Not since the night of the wedding reception. And now they were alone. "Sex."

Funny how a single three-letter word could chase away irritation and replace it with intensity.

"What about it?" he asked.

"Most people these days who discuss marriage, which we did, take it out for a spin. To test compatibility."

"Seems wise." It was the same tone he'd used that night when he gave her fair warning and said the kiss wasn't sudden. That he'd wanted it for a while.

Right here and now was an appropriate time and place for—more stuff. She met his gaze. "Maybe the two of us should have an audition."

"I'm very much in favor of that."

Chapter Twelve

Faith's heart was beating so fast the blood pounded in her ears as Sam took her hands in his and tugged her to a standing position. He slid his arms around her waist and pulled her close to his body. It was amazing how well they fit together and her pulse stuttered at the way his eyes blazed with need.

For her.

"I've been hoping you didn't change your mind." His voice was husky.

"I usually don't once it's made up."

"A woman who knows what she wants is just about as sexy as it gets."

"It's not that I don't appreciate the compliment," she said, "but I really wish you'd kiss me now."

"That would be my pleasure."

Sam barely touched his mouth to hers and every part of her that wasn't already feeling alive kicked into high gear. Her skin tingled, her nerve endings sparked and she could barely breathe. The pressure was soft and slow at first, then he traced the tip of his tongue to the seam of her lips and she opened to him, eager and excited. He delved inside, thoroughly exploring and enticing. He kissed her, open-mouthed and in command. He kissed her lips, then moved to her neck and finally returned to her mouth, as if he were a starving man.

He went on kissing her as if this was all they could do and hadn't already agreed that "stuff" was going to happen. And it didn't, until he finally moved one hand underneath her T-shirt, stroking the bare skin at her waist, setting her whole body on fire. Suddenly her breast was in his palm and even through her plain cotton bra she could feel that there was nothing plain about the sensuous shock waves rolling through her. She went weak with wanting and clung to him.

"I think we should take this upstairs." There was a needy edge to his voice that thrilled.

"Your room or mine?" Faith felt sizzle in places that hadn't sizzled for a very long time. Hormones were bubbling over as if to say, *What took you so long?* "For what it's worth, I vote yours. I've never seen it."

Amusement and wonder chased away the lust in his eyes for just a moment. "Never? Not even a peek? When I wasn't here? You weren't curious?"

"Of course I was." She shivered when he put both hands on the bare skin at her waist. "But it felt like an invasion of your privacy. And therefore wrong."

His mouth curved up in a tender smile. "Like I said. A woman with integrity."

"It's a dirty job but someone has to do it. I—"

He touched a finger to her lips, stopping the flow of words. "Right now I'm seeing that your biggest flaw is talking too much."

"Your room it is." She made a motion across her mouth as if zipping it closed.

His response was to take her hand and lead her up the stairs to the room she had never seen. It was spacious, with a conversation area made up of love seat, chair and ottoman in front of a flat-screen TV. There were two large walk-in closets, presumably a his and hers set. Right now the hers was empty.

There was a king-size bed in dark cherrywood and, while she looked around, he folded down the comforter, blanket and sheet. He'd opened one of the nightstands and now there was a square packet ready and waiting on top of it.

Faith stood in front of him and said, "I like the sleigh bed. It's oddly romantic."

"Why odd? I can be romantic. You should know that better than anyone, plant lady."

Now that she thought about it… "You're right. A first-date flower is a twelve on the one-to-ten romantic scale."

He frowned suddenly. "I should have a rose for you."

"It's okay." She moved closer to him and pulled his shirt from the waistband of his jeans. She touched the first button and undid it, then moved on to the next. When his chest was revealed, she settled her hands on his bare skin, loving the hard contours and the masculine dusting of hair. Her insides turned to liquid heat when she pushed the material from his wide shoulders. "You had me at 'takeout.'"

He swallowed hard. "Just this second I figured out that you have another flaw."

"Is it serious?" She put her fingers on his belt buckle.

"No," he said in a strangled voice. "Definitely fixable."

"Whatever could it be?"

"You have too many clothes on."

That was all it took. He kissed her and in the next instant he had her shirt and bra off without ever taking his mouth from hers. Their labored breathing was loud in the large room as they undressed then fell slowly onto the bed with arms around each other.

He hovered over her, nibbling, taking and giving. Mouths, teeth and tongues nipped and dueled, advanced and retreated. She felt him touch her everywhere and when she was absolutely certain that she couldn't stand it one more second, he reached for the condom and put it on.

Then he levered himself over her, taking his weight on his forearms as he slowly entered her. Her fingers dug into his muscular back as his body pressed deeply into hers. Over and over, a tight, powerful, wonderful intrusion.

The exquisite torment drove her higher and higher still, until behind her eyelids there was an explosion of brightness, not unlike fireworks on the Fourth of July. Pleasure rolled through her and Sam held her as the sweet spasms peaked and slowly faded. Then he started to move again. His hips drove deeper, thrusting once, twice, then…

He went still, pressing his face into her neck and groaning. His muscles convulsed and his big body shuddered. Faith held him close as their breathing returned to normal.

Finally he lifted his head and studied her, an assessing look. "Hi there."

"Hello yourself." She smiled. "And before you ask, I have to say that could not have been more perfect."

A slow, sexy grin turned up the corners of his mouth. "I wasn't going to ask."

"But you were thinking about it. I could hear the wheels turning."

"Ah. Good to know that reading minds is your superpower."

"If only. It's more an intuition thing."

He brushed the hair back from her face and softly touched his mouth to hers. "What is it telling you now?"

She shivered and almost couldn't form a coherent

thought. At the last minute she pulled herself together. "I think you want dessert now."

He smiled, then pressed a kiss to the swell of her breast. "Correct me if I'm wrong, but what we just did felt pretty sweet to me."

"I couldn't agree more, but I was talking about the chocolate cake from the Harvest Café. For your information, I have had it. And I would very much like some now."

"Someone craving sugar?"

"Let's call it a renewing of energy." Playfully she dragged a finger over his collarbone and down his chest. "For later."

"Have I told you how very much I admire the way you think?"

"Yes."

They got out of bed and dressed—sort of. She put on her panties and his long-sleeved shirt, wrinkled from landing in a heap on the floor. He pulled on jeans and fished an old, threadbare T-shirt from a drawer. In the kitchen he got out the single, mile-high slice of cake for them to share and one fork to eat it with. She sat on his lap and he fed her.

She moaned at the burst of wonderfulness on her tongue. "This is better than sex."

"Whoa—" He held the fork out of reach and gave her a faux-outraged look. "Really?"

"That was too easy. And, seriously, you should have led with decadent dessert. Romancing me afterward..." She tsked.

"If memory serves, you were the one who brought up sex. And were, dare I say it, impatient to move things along."

"If I cop to that, can I have my cake?" she said, pointing to the morsel he was holding away from her.

"Yes, you may."

"Okay. What happened in your bedroom was all my

fault." She opened her mouth and he obliged. "Remind me to tell Lucy that her cake works quite efficiently as an interrogation technique."

Having worked up an appetite, they finished dessert in record time and Faith sighed. "That was really good."

"So was the first dessert."

"I agree." She sighed and slid her arms around his neck, then rested her forehead to his temple.

So sex had happened in spite of all the lectures she'd given herself. And here she was sitting on his lap, teasing and talking just like always, though a tad more intimately than before. That didn't mean anything had to change. They were friends and would stay that way, even after she moved out. Which reminded her. "Alex called me today."

"What about?"

"The inspection on my house went well. It's structurally sound, just like you thought. He's brought on more help because there's a lot of work here after the fire and repairs should start soon. Alex thinks the process will go quickly."

"So it's all good."

"Yes. I'll be able to move back in sooner than expected. Seems a fair quid pro quo since I stayed longer than anticipated. But it means I'll be out of your hair before you know it."

His body seemed to tense. "For the record, you haven't been so bad."

"That's nice of you to say, but I know we've been an inconvenience."

"Not really." His arms tightened around her. "Why is there never a construction delay when you really want one?"

She laughed. "You're sweet to try and make me feel better. But the sooner we get back to our place, the sooner you can recover your routine. We wouldn't want to wear out our welcome."

Or, she thought, risk this interlude turning into something more than either of them wanted it to be.

"This was fun, Mommy." Phoebe sat in the passenger seat of the van. "But I wish Sam came with us."

"Seriously?" Faith glanced at her daughter. They were driving home from the Vista Valley mall, a good-size shopping center an hour away from Blackwater Lake. "Do you really think Sam would have enjoyed digging through piles of jeans or racks of tops?"

"Yes. Because he likes hanging out with me."

"That's true. Who wouldn't? You are an awesome kid. But guys aren't really good shoppers."

"Sam might be."

"I wouldn't bet on it, kiddo."

"Did you ask him to come?"

Faith glanced over again. Why wouldn't she let this go? "Actually, no, I didn't."

"How come?"

If only this was one of those questions where she could simply pull rank and say *because I'm the mom*. That was less complicated than the truth. Which was that it crossed her mind to invite him but they'd had sex a couple nights ago and she was doing her darnedest to pretend nothing had changed. She'd give herself an A for effort, but everything felt different.

She smiled more. Her heart did a little involuntary dance every time she saw Sam no matter how hard she tried to keep it from happening. When he looked at her there was a secret in his eyes, a memory of the intimacy they'd shared. But nothing would come of it, which was impossible to explain to an eight-year-old.

"First of all, I didn't invite Sam because he would be bored. And second, this is our special day. A tradition.

You and I have shopped for school clothes together since you were in kindergarten."

"That's really nice, Mom." Neither road noise nor radio muffled the big sigh coming from the passenger seat. "But I really missed Sam. And I bet he was lonely without us today."

Wasn't the mother supposed to guilt the child? Now Faith felt as if she'd slapped the man who took them in. And he had looked awfully wistful when they'd headed out for the mall earlier.

"I'm sure he found something to do." Faith put as much cheer in her voice as she could manage. It was a challenge, what with feeling petty and selfish. "And we're almost ho— I mean back."

She'd nearly said *home*. But that was just a saying, right? It didn't have any deeper meaning.

Her cell phone was sitting in the console between the seats and signaled an incoming text message.

"I'll get it, Mommy. You're not supposed to look at your phone when you're driving."

"Okay." The kid probably knew more about the device anyway. Hopefully in a few years when Phoebe was behind the wheel, she'd remember what she just said.

Phoebe picked it up. "It's from Sam. He made barbecued chicken for dinner. He wants to know if you want rice or potatoes."

If they hadn't slept together she wouldn't have thought twice about that question. It would be no big deal. But somehow she was reading something into the question. "Tell him rice."

Phoebe's fingers moved over the keys and then she waited. Several moments later there was a signal. She read the message and giggled. Faith's stomach knotted. She hoped he hadn't said something meant only for her, something that her daughter shouldn't read. That was different because of sex.

"What is it?" she demanded.

"Don't be mad, Mommy. I answered that you wanted ice cream. Sam knew it was me."

Oh, thank God. "So text him back and say rice."

"I don't have to. He said he'll surprise us. Maybe with dessert."

The way to a woman's heart... It was much less complicated when the female in question was eight. He'd fed Faith chocolate cake *after* she gave herself to him. What did that mean?

Ten minutes later when they walked in the door with some of the bags, Sam was waiting. He whistled at the volume. "Did you buy out the store?"

"No, silly." Phoebe set her bag down and gave him a hug. "But there's more in the car. We couldn't bring everything in."

"I'll go get it," he volunteered. "Carrying stuff is men's work."

"Don't forget," Faith warned, "that most of her clothes were ruined because of the fire."

"I'm not judging." Sam moved close and the look in his eyes felt like a caress.

"And I needed a few things, too." Her heart two-stepped at the heat from his body. "I'm not going to even think about how much I spent until the bill comes."

"Keep in mind that your insurance will cover the replacement cost of your belongings. I looked over your policy and it's a good one."

The simple reassurance was something Faith was still getting used to. She didn't expect support because she'd never had it from anyone besides Aunt Cathy. You couldn't miss what you'd never had.

She smiled up at him. "I'd forgotten about that. Thanks for helping me justify all of this."

"Happy to be of help."

Phoebe was looking at them, a puzzled expression on her face. "Are we gonna unload the car? I'm starving."

"At your service, General." He gave her a small salute.

"I'm not a general."

"You give orders like one." He walked by Faith and their shoulders brushed, on purpose most likely.

When all the bags had been carried inside and dropped at the bottom of the stairs to be dealt with later, the three of them worked together in the kitchen, putting the finishing touches on dinner. Phoebe set the table. Faith put together a salad and Sam heated frozen potatoes in the oven. So much for rice. He knew her little girl loved French fries. When all the food was set out they took their usual places at the table.

Sam picked up the platter of chicken and held it out to Phoebe. "The drumsticks are all yours, Squirt."

"That's my favorite." She looked at him as if he'd hung the moon.

"Your turn," he said to Faith, the platter in one hand, tongs in the other.

She took the tool from him and their fingers brushed. The touch sizzled straight through her but somehow she managed to put a piece of chicken on her plate.

"You're supposed to say thank you, Mom." Phoebe gave her a look. "That's what you always tell me."

"You're right. How could I forget?" She saw Sam smile and the knowing look in his eyes said he knew exactly why she'd forgotten. And that he'd be more than happy to make her forget anytime.

"May I have some French fries?" Phoebe asked politely.

"Sure." Sam picked up the plate so that she could serve herself.

"You need salad, too," Faith reminded her daughter when there was a very generous portion in front of her.

"I will," the little girl assured her. "But I have to eat some stuff first to make room on my plate."

Sam made a sound and Faith shot him a warning look that said he better not laugh and, to his credit, he didn't. He got points for that. As a mother Faith had learned there were some hills to die on, but this wasn't one of them.

When everyone had a full plate, they started eating and Phoebe wasn't the only one who was hungry. The chicken was cooked to perfection, not dry or burned. But it was messy. Faith wiped her face.

"You've got some sauce—" He pointed to her mouth, then picked up one of the extra napkins on the table and brushed it over her lips. "There."

"Thanks." Faith smiled. Then she noticed her daughter taking it all in and got a bad feeling something was coming. It didn't take long to find out she was right.

"Mommy, are you going out with Sam?"

How she wanted to simply say it was complicated, but that wouldn't stop Phoebe. Apparently she'd become aware of the intimate shift between her and Sam. If she hadn't underestimated this child's ability to pick up the vibes going on around her, she'd have been prepared with an answer. But now she had to wing it. No pun intended to the chicken.

Faith gave Sam an apologetic look, but he didn't seem upset at all. More amused than anything and, dare she say, eager to let her field the question.

Kids were nothing if not literal and that's how she decided to approach the response. "Sam and I have never gone out."

He nodded as if to say that was technically true. Although technically sex made it a debatable distinction. At least she wasn't one of his first-date-rose girls.

"Is he your boyfriend?"

"We have never talked about it." Again Faith decided to go with a literal truth. It was a Hail Mary pass because she knew her daughter and that wasn't going to fly.

The little girl looked more curious, if that were possible. And determined. She turned to Sam. "Do you like my mom?"

"I like her very much," he said without hesitation.

"Mom, do you like Sam?"

She'd liked him the first time he bought a rose from her and that hadn't changed. Although since living in his house, she'd found out he wasn't the shallow play-the-field kind of guy she had teased him about being. He was kind, caring and generous and she liked him even more.

"Yes," she said, "I like Sam."

"Are you getting married?"

Oh, boy. Now it was really uncomfortable. At least the truth was simple and easy. "No—"

"How would you feel about it if we did?" Sam interrupted her to ask Phoebe.

"Well—" She stuffed a French fry into her mouth. "If that meant you could be my dad, I would really like it."

He smiled affectionately. "So you approve of me for your mom?"

"Yes."

"That's good to know." All traces of amusement were gone and Sam looked dead serious. "How about this? If your mom and I decide to get married, you will be the very first to know."

"Do you promise?"

He made an X on the left side of his chest. "Cross my heart."

"Okay."

That seemed to satisfy her because the inquisition

stopped. But Faith was curious now. Apparently Phoebe had inherited inquisitiveness from her.

On the one hand, Sam's direct approach had stopped the awkward questions. He'd done it to distract and the strategy was pretty darn smart. That had to be why he'd said what he had. She couldn't imagine any other reason for him to confirm Phoebe's approval.

In spite of their "what if" discussion about marriage, Faith couldn't believe he was serious about taking that step. If she'd learned anything from selling flowers to him all these months, it was that Sam was all about the chase. Because Faith was a challenge it made her intriguing to him.

Surely that's all it was. When she moved back to her house, things would go back to the way they were. In the meantime they were friends with benefits.

Chapter Thirteen

"Phoebe, it's bath time." For the two weeks since school had started, Faith walked into the family room at the same time every night and issued this order.

Sam had mixed feelings. He enjoyed watching television or playing video games with this little girl but watching the imaginative ways she tried to wiggle out of the bedtime routine was pretty entertaining, too. By far his favorite part of the day was later, when more often than not he took Faith to his bed. If he was dissatisfied about anything, it was that she never stayed through the night. She didn't want her very perceptive daughter to pick up on how much things had changed, what with them sleeping together.

"But, Mom, me and Sam are watching this show." She was curled up against him on the leather couch and burrowed in a little deeper.

"It's recorded," he told her. "We can finish it tomorrow."

"Whose side are you on?" Phoebe frowned up at him.

He felt a tug in the region of his heart at the look that

was so much like her mother. "I don't take sides. I'm neutral. Like Switzerland."

"What does that even mean?" the little girl asked.

He used the remote to shut off the TV. "I'll explain in the morning."

"Good answer." Faith smiled her approval. "Well done."

"I'm learning the ropes."

"What if I forget to ask about it in the morning?" Phoebe insisted.

"I'll remind you," he promised.

"What if you forget?"

"I'll write myself a note and leave it by the coffeepot."

She thought about that, then nodded. "You and Mommy both drink coffee so I guess someone will remember."

"Crisis averted," Faith said. "Let's go. You need to wash your hair tonight."

"But it gets all tangled," she complained.

"I have a spray that gets all the snarls out."

"But it hurts when you comb it."

"I'll be gentle," she promised.

Phoebe stood and folded her arms over her chest. "I don't want to wash my hair."

Her mother didn't back down. "Really? I never would have guessed."

"You're gonna make me anyway, right?"

"I see you've met me," Faith said drily. "The alternative is greasy hair that will start to smell and get bugs. There goes your friends, invitations to birthday parties and social life. You'll be stuck with just me."

And me, Sam wanted to say. But he didn't have the right.

"You're exaggerating, Mommy."

"No."

"Sam?" The little girl looked at him. "If I don't wash my hair would it smell so bad I couldn't stay here with you?"

The question of staying with him had crossed his mind

a lot as the repairs on their house progressed. Every day of work on it was a day closer to them leaving. The thought of this big house without them in it wasn't pretty.

"You can stay with me no matter what." He shrugged when Faith gave him a look. "But at school they might have something to say about it."

"I hate school anyway." Her little face settled into a pout. "But if I don't go, the sheriff will take Mommy to jail."

"Oh?" One of his eyebrows rose as he looked at Faith trying not to laugh.

"We've had this conversation before. About hating school," she explained.

"I figured."

"Sam—" There was an "aha" tone in Phoebe's voice. "'No matter what' means I could stay with you if they put Mommy in jail, right?"

Caught between a rock and a hard place. The kid had a future in litigation. Lawyers got paid to make an argument and Phoebe was a natural.

"That's right, Sam. A promise is a promise. She could stay with you." Faith was enjoying this way too much.

No fair. Two against one, he wanted to say, but he was no coward. Crisis defined character and he would show the women what he was made of.

"You could absolutely live here with me," he agreed enthusiastically. "But you should keep this in mind. I can't leave you alone when I go to work and since the school has declared your hair a health hazard, you'd have to come to the office with me."

"That would be fun." The kid tried to brazen it out but didn't look completely sure about that.

"I think so, too," he said. "You can watch while I work on the computer."

"Don't you do other stuff?" she asked hopefully.

"Oh, sure." He thought for a moment. "Sometimes I have meetings with clients. We talk about interest rates on loans, money, the stock market. You'll like it."

"Boring." She heaved a big sigh. "Okay. I'll go take a bath and wash my hair."

"Good call," he said to her.

She came over to give him a hug. "'Night, Sam."

"Sleep tight." He held her close for a moment, then saw Faith give him two thumbs-up.

He couldn't ever remember feeling so much pride in an accomplishment before. Especially the part where Faith approved of his crisis management. The ladies headed out of the room and up the stairs and then he was alone.

At least sounds from upstairs drifted to him. Running water. Muted voices. Giggling. Family sounds. And they wouldn't be here much longer.

He knew how emptiness felt but it was bigger now because he'd experienced the opposite. He liked the opposite very much.

His bar had an exceptional bottle of Scotch and this seemed like a very good time to have some. He poured the amber liquid into a tumbler and walked outside, leaving the French door ajar. The yard was lit up like a football stadium with lights outlining the boundaries and the crystal clear water of the pool. He sat at the patio table and let the memories wash over him.

Faith smiling as she watched while he let Phoebe splash him in the pool. Faith talking to his sister and looking very serious about something. Faith laughing and sexy. In his arms and his bed.

They talked for hours and had a lot in common. It was good between them, really good. Surely she felt it, too.

He didn't want what they had, the intimacy they shared, to change. He liked things just the way they were and if she moved back to her house...

"Sam?"

He glanced over his shoulder and she was there with her hand on the French door. A feeling squeezed tight in his chest, something very close to pain, and yet he was able to smile. "Hi. Is Phoebe settled?"

"Clean hair and all." She laughed. "You were so great with her. I think that discussion of consequences wore her down. She was practically asleep before her head hit the pillow."

"Happy to help."

She came over to stand beside him. "What are you doing out here all by yourself?"

"Drinking." He held up the glass, which still had the same amount of Scotch in it. "Maybe a little brooding."

"Ooh, you'll want to be alone for that."

"No." Actually alone wasn't the problem. He was fine by himself. It's just that he was better with her. He reached out and gently took her hand. "Stay."

"Are you sure?"

"Very."

"Okay." She sat in the chair next to his. "So, what are you brooding about?"

"We haven't talked about—us." He felt her tense even though their bodies weren't touching.

"Sam, I—"

"Look, you've been avoiding the subject ever since Phoebe asked if I was your boyfriend."

"Yeah."

How like her to answer honestly. It was one of his favorite things about her. "The fact that she noticed a difference just blew me away. I had no idea she was so perceptive."

"Kids pick up on cues from everyone around them." The shadows in her eyes made it obvious she was remembering her childhood and the loneliness of being shut out.

The last thing Sam wanted to do was make her sad. "Did you ever define for her what we are?"

"How could I when it's not clear to me?" She held up her hand to signal that she wasn't finished. "And that's fine. I'm okay with this. One day at a time works."

"I would be, too, if you weren't leaving soon."

"I'm not going to Mars," she teased.

"Funny girl."

"We'll still see each other, I hope."

"Count on it," he said firmly. "But it won't be the same."

"No. Won't it be better from your perspective?"

"How do you figure?" he asked.

"No more going through bedtime rebellion and negotiation."

"It's one of the best parts of my day. I can't wait to see what she comes up with next." He smiled wistfully. "And it's a risk/reward thing. I came out pretty good with a hug."

"Trust me. It gets old," Faith said ruefully.

"Maybe. But the alternative would be no hug at all."

"Sam, you can see her anytime you want."

"It won't be the same." He met her gaze. "Not like having you here."

"What are you saying?"

Pieces of an idea had been rolling around in his head since Phoebe had asked for clarification on their relationship. Everything came together now. "You like me, right?"

"Yes." She didn't look happy about it so the response was her being scrupulously honest again.

"And I like you." It seemed like a no-brainer to him. "I think we should make this arrangement permanent."

"You mean just stay here and live with you?"

"Yes." He thought about how that sounded and added, "Of course we'd get married."

She blinked. "We'll do what now?"

Sam studied her expression, trying to decide if she was

happy surprised or just shocked. Well, he was kind of surprised, too, that the words had come out of his mouth, but as the idea hung in the air between them it felt completely right.

"It's not like we haven't talked about it," he pointed out.

"That was a hypothetical discussion."

"You agreed all the reasons in the 'for' column were practical. And positive. Don't you like it here?"

"I love it." She caught the corner of her top lip between her teeth. "Still, Sam—"

"Phoebe's on board," he reminded her.

"That could be all about the pool." She smiled. "But something tells me she's a yes vote."

"Things are pretty great. And we could go on just the way we are."

"It has been pretty perfect," she admitted. "But you must have a flaw."

"Persistence."

She laughed. "And that means what?"

"I don't give up. Not when I think something is right. And I feel that way about this. Marry me, Faith."

She thought for several moments. "So you're not going to give up?"

"No."

"We'll have to talk to Phoebe about it. Include her in all discussions."

"Of course," he said. "We'll do it in the morning. Maybe she'll forget to ask about Switzerland. What do you say, Faith? Do you trust me?"

"Yes."

"Okay then." He leaned close and kissed her. "We're having a wedding."

Today Faith was going to marry Sam Hart.

It had been ten days since he'd asked her. True to his

word, Phoebe was the first to know and she'd enthusiastically embraced the plan and couldn't wait until everything was official. Last night he'd spent the night at his sister's and today they were meeting him at the Blackwater Lake courthouse. She felt as if she was going to throw up.

"Mommy, can you help me with my dress?"

She turned and saw her pretty little girl in the doorway. They'd spent another fun mother/daughter day at the mall buying new dresses for the occasion. The difference was that this time Sam had come along.

"Of course. Come here." The little girl walked over to her, then turned her back.

Faith took the ends of the cream satin ribbons that trailed behind and tied them. The dress was full, pink and had dainty rosebuds on the bodice. She took her time fluffing the loops of the bow until they were perfect. Keeping her hands busy almost hid the fact that they were shaking.

Finally satisfied, she gave the bow a pat. "All done."

Phoebe turned. And held the sides of her dress out. "How do I look?"

Faith studied the full effect—new, shiny patent leather shoes and pink socks with lacy edges. The sides of her blond hair were pulled back from her face and fastened at her crown with a rose clip while fat curls tumbled down her back.

"You look so beautiful everyone will think you're the bride."

"You're silly, Mom. I'm not old enough to get married."

"True. And you won't be until you're thirty-five."

"That's so *old*," Phoebe protested.

It probably seemed that way when you were eight. At Phoebe's age Faith was just beginning to realize that her parents belonged to a club that only had two members. Love was their cocoon and Faith was always on the outside looking in.

"Mommy?"

"Hmm?" She shook her head and focused. "What?"

"You look funny. Are you okay?"

She would be as soon as she saw Sam. He was the best man she'd ever known and just thinking about him made her heart beat faster. They *were* good together. "I'm fine. How do I look?"

The two of them stood side by side in front of the mirrored closet door. Faith studied her reflection—the powder blue column dress and matching three-inch heels. Her blond hair parted on the side and pulled back from her face into a messy side bun. In her ears she wore the diamond studs that were Sam's wedding gift to her and around her neck dangled the white gold, heart-shaped locket with pictures of her parents inside that Aunt Cathy had given her.

"Something old, something new, something blue," she said, smoothing the front of her dress.

"What about something borrowed?" Phoebe asked.

Faith had told her about the bridal tradition for luck. "I guess I'll have to skip that one."

"No. I'll find something—" The little girl ran out of the room.

"It's okay, Phoebs—" A text signal interrupted her. It was from the limousine driver. Sam had ordered a car that would take them to the courthouse. It was on-site and ready to go when she was.

"Phoebe," she called out. "We have to go."

"But I hafta find something you can borrow." The voice was muffled.

Faith stood in the doorway of the child's room where it looked as if a tornado had recently touched down. She made a mental note to deal with it after the wedding. *Oh, God...* She was getting married. The knots in her stomach pulled tighter.

"Phoebe, there's no time. The car is here. Sam is waiting."

"But, Mommy—"

"Let's go."

"I found it!" The little girl emerged from her closet holding up a bracelet of clear beads she'd made at summer camp. She handed it over. "Something borrowed."

"I'll put it on in the car," she promised, hustling them both down the stairs.

Outside there was a black town car parked in front of the house. A very handsome thirtysomething man wearing a dark suit and conservative tie stood beside it. He opened the rear passenger door for them.

"My name is Mike. I'm taking you to the courthouse, right?"

"Yes."

"I got a new dress," Phoebe informed him.

"It's very pretty."

"Mommy and me had to get new clothes for the wedding because our house was in the fire."

"I'm sorry to hear that," the driver said.

"It's okay. Now we live with Sam and Mommy's gonna get married to him."

"So I heard." He smiled and looked at Faith. "Congratulations."

"Thank you. Get in, Phoebe."

"But I'm talkin' to Mike."

"And Sam is waiting," she said for the second time.

"Okay." Phoebe gave the driver a little wave then climbed into the backseat.

Faith followed and slid onto the cushy leather, sinking into it a little. After closing the door behind her, the driver got in and started the car, then headed out to the street. The ride was so smooth it was almost like floating on air.

"Mommy?"

There was a questioning look on the little girl's face, as if this luxury car was a sign that things were about to change in a really significant way. That realization hit Faith as if she'd walked full speed into a clear glass door without seeing it.

"What is it, Phoebe?" she asked gently.

"After you marry Sam are you gonna sleep in his room?"

"Why do you ask?" She wasn't stalling exactly. This was called getting context to help frame her answer.

"My friend Christie's mom and dad are married and they sleep in the same bed. I just wondered if you and Sam are gonna do that."

It was a straightforward question and deserved the same back. "Yes."

Phoebe's forehead puckered with concern. "What if I have a bad dream?"

"I'm not sure what you mean, sweetie."

"Well, when I have one now, you let me get in bed with you. After you and Sam get married, can I still sleep with you? If I'm scared?"

"Of course you can. Nothing's going to change." Even as the words tumbled out of her mouth, Faith knew they were a lie.

Everything was going to be different. By definition a husband and wife were a unit and there would be consequences for her daughter. Faith flashed back to how lonely and isolated her childhood had been and never wanted her child to feel that way. Sam had a big, magnetic personality. He was the kind of man who was consuming.

The kind of man who'd made her forget everything but a future with him. They were on the outskirts of town now and would be at the courthouse shortly.

Faith remembered how perfectly her mother and father completed each other with nothing left over for anyone else. Whether or not it had been deliberate, she'd felt cast aside. She'd sworn that if she ever had a baby, she would give everything she had and her child would never come last. But just a while ago she'd been impatient with Phoebe because Sam was waiting.

Was this the beginning of breaking that solemn promise she'd made?

The driver pulled to a stop in front of the ordinary building in downtown Blackwater Lake where official business was conducted. Mike got out of the car and came around to the sidewalk, then opened the door.

"Here we are," he announced.

"Thank you." Faith slid out and waited for Phoebe to follow.

"Sam gave me orders to wait," the driver said.

Faith barely heard because the blood was pounding in her ears and she felt sick to her stomach. She clutched the bracelet in one hand and her child with the other then walked inside. The public area was deserted as it was nearly closing time but there was an information window straight ahead.

The two of them stopped in front of it. "I'm looking for Sam Hart—"

"You must be Faith." The woman smiled. "The wedding party is in Judge Hewlett's office. It's just down the hall. Sam said to send you back when you arrived. He's a hottie. You're a lucky girl."

He was definitely hot, but she wasn't feeling all that lucky.

Down a short hall, the office door was open and there were people inside—Ellie and Alex. The mayor and her husband. Linc, Rose, his parents. The judge. And Sam.

A short while ago Faith had been so sure she'd be okay when she saw him, but now not so much. It confirmed her worst fears. He was more handsome than ever in a dark suit and red silk tie. As always, her heart skipped a beat at the sight of him and she wished that wasn't so.

Probably she greeted everyone but she wasn't sure.

They said she and Phoebe looked beautiful, then Sam took her hand.

He searched her face. "You're white as a sheet. Is everything all right?"

When did he get to know her so well? She shook her head. "No."

"Tell me."

"I c-can't go through with this—" Her voice caught.

"We'll be right back," he said to the people over his shoulder, then tugged her into the hall. "What is it?"

"Phoebe has to come first."

"That goes without saying," he assured her.

"You don't understand. I can't marry you."

Disbelief and confusion pooled in his eyes. "This is about what your parents did to you, right?"

"I can't take a chance." She clutched the bracelet Phoebe had made tightly in her hand. "I just can't, Sam. Love is not what—"

"No one said anything about love." There was frustration in his voice.

No one had said the word, but that didn't make it any less true. She was in love with Sam Hart. Because the feeling was bigger and more powerful than she'd ever believed possible, she had to walk away from him.

She should never have agreed to marry him. She should never have trusted the moonlight. Faith's first mistake had been falling in love with him. Her second was being caught up in the romance. Marrying Sam would make it a trilogy of errors but for Phoebe's sake that wasn't going to happen.

And her heart was breaking.

Chapter Fourteen

Sam followed Faith back into the office where people were gathered to watch him marry her. She was going for her daughter and he expected her to leave without a word. That's not what happened.

She took Phoebe's hand into her own trembling one, then turned to face everyone. "I'm so sorry to have inconvenienced you all. But there's not going to be a wedding today—" Her voice broke and after a deep, shuddering breath she met his gaze. Softly, as if only to him, she said, "I'm so very sorry."

Phoebe protested when she headed for the door. "Mommy, stop—"

"We have to go, sweetie."

"But we're gonna marry Sam—"

And then they were gone, the sound of footsteps and fading voices echoing on the linoleum floor and all the way down the hall. Sam felt as if someone had slugged him in the gut with a sledgehammer. All kinds of things raced through his mind, including that he was glad his brother Cal hadn't been able to break away from work to be here on such short notice. But the rest of the family was staring at him, waiting for an explanation. If only he had one that made sense.

"Sam, I know that look—" Katherine Hart moved closer and put her hand on his arm. "What's going on?"

"You heard her." There was bitterness in his tone that he couldn't manage to suppress. "No wedding. And don't ask me why. I don't understand it myself."

That was true. He knew what she just said and what she'd told him about her parents but he hadn't realized how deeply she felt about it. This was not how he'd expected the day to go and losing her cut deep.

"Honey, there must be something you can do." There was a maternal look in his mother's eyes and that was dangerous.

Sam knew she wanted to hug him and make it all better, but this wasn't a boo boo she could kiss away. "Mom, don't—"

"What, sweetheart?" There was pity in her eyes.

"And don't look at me that way."

"Is there anything we can do, son?" His father carefully hid whatever he was feeling. There was only a man-to-man look in his eyes that said he got how tough this was.

"I don't think so, Dad." Sam glanced at everyone else and his expression must have warned them not to say anything. Fortunately they didn't, apparently okay with letting the folks handle it.

"What did Faith say to you?" His mother glanced at his father, as if to ask if the question was permissible in the male world.

"It doesn't matter. She made her point."

"Which was?" Hastings asked.

"She's not into marriage."

Sam remembered her observation that he was adamant about not committing to marriage. She'd teased him about keeping his secret because if that got out it could cramp his style with the single ladies of Blackwater Lake who thought they had a chance to win his affection. Even as he'd said it, he'd known his adamant comment about never getting married fell into the protesting-too-much category. Because there was something about Faith that drew him. And winning her affection had appealed to him from the start.

She was beautiful, but it was more than that. She was smart and sarcastic. The combination was sexy as sin. And there was the fact that she was completely unimpressed by his bank balance, except as it pertained to him being one of her best customers who would fund her daughter's college education.

Sam had never met a woman like her and his feelings had just grown more complicated with her living in his house. He liked her there. He liked Phoebe there. It was the best time of his life and now she'd left him at the altar. Hopes and dreams hit the ground and shattered.

"You're hurting, Sam." His mother's words got through. "Let us help."

"I'm fine."

"You might be able to pull off that lie with someone else, but I'm your mother."

"Do not say that you know me better than I know myself."

"Although that's true," she said, "it's not what I wanted to tell you."

"Then what?"

"It's not necessary to put on a brave front for us. We're your family and can see through it so don't waste the energy."

"Or the time," his dad said. "Go talk to her. She probably went back to the house."

Sam knew he was right. Faith would move out. It wasn't easy for her to take anything she hadn't earned. In his heart he knew she wasn't a user, not the kind of woman who would take from him. So she had to get her things. And Phoebe's, too. The limousine driver had orders to wait and his guess was that she'd told him they wanted to go back.

"You're right, Dad." This could be worked out. He looked at his parents. "I have to go."

"Good luck, son."

Sam had driven himself to the courthouse and the plan had been for his folks to take his car back to Ellie's place where he'd pick it up later. There was a reservation for dinner at the new five-star restaurant just opened at Holden House. That wasn't going to happen.

He retrieved his car from the public building's parking lot and drove back to his house. There were lights on and he felt a tremendous sense of relief. It was a clue how worried he'd been that she might not be here and he wouldn't know where to find her. After parking in the driveway, he let himself in and walked upstairs, past his room, where he'd looked forward to bringing Faith as his wife. But he might still be able to make that happen.

The door to her room was open and she was there, changed out of the dress she'd worn just a little while ago. His gut tightened now the way it had when he'd first seen her in it, so beautiful he'd ached from wanting her. Now she was in jeans and a T-shirt and he still wanted her, maybe even more. But she was busy pulling clothes out of drawers and putting them in a pile on the bed.

"Hi, Faith." He said her name in a firm voice. It hadn't been his intention to startle her. Well, maybe just a little. After all, she'd just made a fool out of him.

She gasped and whirled to face him, hand to her chest. "Sam, I—"

"Didn't expect me?" He smiled but knew it felt stiff and humorless. "Surprise."

She was holding a pair of sweatpants in front of her like a shield. "I didn't think you'd want to see me."

"Surprise again." Struggling for casual, he leaned a shoulder against the doorjamb.

"If you're thinking there's anything more to talk about, you're wrong."

"No, you are. I have several things to say."

"I'm sorry, Sam. I shouldn't have said yes when you asked me to marry you. That was stupid. Really dumb. If I were you, I wouldn't want to marry me."

"But you're not me."

She glanced at the dresser. "The ring is there."

The fact that he'd been right about her not being grasping and greedy did not ease the bitterness of his anger. But it did nudge him over the edge, into something that he was afraid would hurt a lot more when this conversation ended.

"That's not why I'm here."

"Then say what you have to. Get it off your chest." She straightened, facing him dead-on, bracing herself. "Whatever it is, I deserve it."

"You'll get no argument from me." He didn't move. "Everything was fine. What happened to change your mind?"

"Something Phoebe said." She met his gaze. "She wanted to know if she could come into bed with us if she has a nightmare."

"Of course," he said.

"That's what I told her, but it made me think. And remember. By the time we got there I knew I just couldn't go through with the wedding."

"You're a coward."

Her chin lifted slightly. "I don't deny that. But I'm not afraid for myself. It's Phoebe—"

"Do you really think I'd hurt her?"

"No. Not deliberately, at least. But I can't risk her being hurt. I know what it feels like. The loneliness is—" She pressed her lips together into a straight line. The distress in her eyes was real, palpable.

"We're not them, Faith. We're not your parents. I care about Phoebe and would never shut her out." Now he straightened and took a step forward. "I care about you, too. Very much."

"Sam, you don't get it. Love doesn't bring a man and woman together. It excludes everyone else."

He had to find the words to convince her that if she refused to let herself be happy, her selfish, negligent parents would win. "That doesn't have to be the case."

"But I can't take a chance. Being left out is heartbreaking." She was no longer holding the sweatpants as much as clutching the material in a grip so tight her knuckles turned white. "I know what it's like to be pushed off onto a relative to be raised, even though I had a perfectly good set of parents. Their only excuse for doing that to me was love. They *cared* so much for each other that there was no room for me."

"You and I would never do that to her."

"There are no guarantees."

"Yeah, there are. I wasn't raised like that. No one is left out where I come from. You know about Linc, that he has a different father. He tried to shake off the family, but we wouldn't go for it." He cocked a thumb at himself. "I'm not the kind of guy who leaves anyone out in the cold. Especially a child. We're not them," he said again.

"I am. I have their DNA and they were not very good role models. I have no reference for how to balance love with being a mother."

He blinked at her, suddenly confused. If she was saying what he thought, he might stand a chance. "Let me get this straight. Does that mean you are in love with me?"

She all but winced, as if the truth of those words was like a slap in the face. After a shuddering breath she said, "I'm afraid I am."

"Okay, then." In his mind everything clicked into place. "We can work this out, Faith."

"No." She shook her head. "Phoebe only has me."

"Even if—and this is a big if—we were wrapped up in each other and excluded her, don't you think she would have something to say about it?"

"She shouldn't have to. It's my job to protect her and not let that happen."

"So correct me if I'm wrong. We love each other, but you won't marry me because we *might* screw up?"

"That's not— It sounds so—" She shook her head. "You don't get it."

"I do. It sounds silly because it is. Maybe you should let yourself be happy. If we make a mistake, we'll fix it. On the bright side, we might not screw up. At least not that way."

"No."

"Sam?" That was Phoebe's voice.

He looked down and she was there. He'd been so caught up, he hadn't heard her. There was a shell-shocked, confused expression in her eyes.

He went down on one knee, to her level. "Hey, Squirt."

"Mommy said we're not gonna be able to stay with you anymore."

"That's why I'm here. So we can work things out."

"Phoebe—" Faith's voice was quiet, but firm. "Are your things all together?"

"Yes. But I don't have anything to carry them in."

"Okay. We'll just put them in the van loose."

"But, Mommy, I don't want to leave Sam."

"I know, baby—" Her voice broke then, but moments later she pulled herself together. "Someday you'll understand that this is for the best."

"No, I won't."

"Phoebe, this is something we have to do. Please say goodbye to Sam and thank him for his hospitality."

Tears gathered in the little girl's eyes, then spilled over and down her cheeks. She threw herself against him, her little body trembling. "Thank you for letting me stay with you and use your pool. Bye, S-Sam."

"Don't cry, Phoebs. I'll be seeing you all the time."

"Promise?" She lifted her head and met his gaze.

"Cross my heart." He made the X over the left side of his chest.

"Okay." She shot her mother a glare that was like a deadly death ray, then walked away and slammed the door to her room.

Sam stood and faced Faith. "Even Phoebe knows you don't need to protect her from me. From us."

"She's eight. I'm the adult."

"Doesn't look that way from where I'm standing," he said. That was low but it matched his mood. When a guy got left at the altar maybe he could be cut some slack for being a jerk.

"She's not your child, Sam. She's mine. And this is my decision."

"There's nothing I can say to change your mind." It wasn't a question. He saw the look in her eyes, as if a wall had slammed shut to keep him out.

"No. Nothing."

He stared at her, memorizing the delicate line of her jaw, the sadness in her eyes, then turned away without another word. He left the house, afraid he would say something he shouldn't. Like begging her not to go. He'd come awfully close to doing that.

The hardest part was knowing she loved him. That made things worse because he was in love with her, too. So he just answered his own question. He'd wondered if seeing her would make things worse. The answer was yes.

The next day Sam got home from work as late as possible, but the quiet was as weird and lonely as he'd expected. When Faith and Phoebe had been living here, many evenings he walked in the door before them and, even though no one else was there, he hadn't experienced this particular aloneness. So a shrink would tell him it was all in his head. Maybe, partly, that was true, but mostly it was in his heart. He missed the hell out of them.

Because he was a glutton for punishment, he walked through the house and let memories scroll through his mind. From the family room he could see the pool where he and Phoebe had so much fun while Faith laughed at their antics. Playing video games and talking to the little girl about strategies to deal with bullying.

Last night he'd slept fitfully on the couch in here because he couldn't stomach the memories he'd have sleeping in the bed where he'd made love to Faith. In the entryway he reached down to pick up what turned out to be a sock that must have fallen when Phoebe carried her things to the van. It was a little pink one with a lace edge. That was when a couple of things hit him simultaneously.

As much as he wanted to right this minute, he couldn't take this sock to Phoebe because he didn't know where Faith had gone. He would do it tomorrow at her flower stand in the lobby of the bank building. That would be an excuse to see her. The second thing was very shrink-worthy. He couldn't be in this house. At least not right now.

When a guy absolutely, positively needed to go somewhere there was food, entertainment and no family to pity him, it had to be Bar None.

He grabbed his keys and left the big, lonely house. Fifteen minutes later he'd passed through downtown Blackwater Lake then pulled into the bar's parking lot. The place was like an old pair of sneakers—comfortable and dependable. Over the roof there was the neon sign with crossed cocktail glasses and in the window by the heavy door the word *Beer* was spelled out in yellow lights. Both invited a person to come inside for a cold one and that's exactly what he wanted.

There were booths around the exterior of the room and bistro tables scattered over the rest of the wooden floor not designated for dancing. Straight ahead was the bar with brass foot rail and padded stools in front of it. There was a seat at the end all by itself with Sam's name on it.

He'd barely sat down when the redheaded owner moved in front of him. "Hey. How's it going?"

"Can't complain." Delanie Carlson had pity in her blue eyes. "You?"

Sam was here to ignore his feelings not talk about them. So he lied. "Great."

"What can I get you?"

"Beer. Tap. And keep them coming."

She nodded, then grabbed a frosted glass mug and put it under a spout before expertly drawing the golden liquid with just enough foam on the top. She set a cocktail napkin in front of him on the scarred wooden bar and placed the glass on it.

"Thanks." He took a long drink and let the ice-cold effervescence spill through him, hoping it would numb every feeling in its wake.

Delanie was watching him closely. "I haven't seen you in here for a while. Not since before the fire."

Sam knew she really meant before Faith. Or maybe he only thought that because she was all he could think about. He took another long drink and tried to figure out whether to answer or just ignore the question. That was rude, so he finally decided and said, "It has been a while. What's new with you?"

"Same old, same old." Her eyes narrowed as he drained the glass.

"Can I get another one?" he asked pleasantly.

"Sure thing." But pity was replaced by concern in those pretty eyes of hers before she set a fresh frosty glass in front of him.

The scrutiny was a little annoying when he just wanted to be left alone. "Maybe you should just bring me a pitcher."

"Drink that one first. Maybe a little slower this time," she said, glancing at the mug. "Then we'll talk about why you're determined to tie one on."

"I'm simply here to relax." Because his house wasn't a haven anymore. He knew the pleasant tone he was going for had slipped a little.

"Okay." She tilted her head and the ends of her sassy, red-haired ponytail brushed the shoulder of her T-shirt. "But I'm keeping an eye on you."

He nodded, then glared at her back until she disappeared into the room behind the bar where her office was located. The next time Sam saw his sister, he planned to have a sternly worded conversation with her. When she'd told him Blackwater Lake was the best place ever to live, she'd left out the part where a guy couldn't have a good brood at the local bar without being hovered over.

And speaking of hovering… Thirty minutes after thinking that thought, the sister in question walked into the establishment with their brother Linc. Both of them walked straight over to him. Without a word, she grabbed his nearly-empty third beer and brought it over to a bistro table where she sat down. Linc followed her and both of them looked at him—a dare in their eyes. He tried to signal Delanie to get another one, but she was at the other end of the bar. Her back was to him and all signs pointed to her deliberately ignoring him.

"Oh, for crying out loud…" He slid off his bar stool and walked over to the table. After sitting on the third chair at the table, he liberated his beer. "I'm not finished with that."

"I'm driving you home," Ellie said.

"Okay." He'd been planning to find a ride, so that declaration just made his life easier. Maybe. But when he met her gaze reality sank in. Nope, he was going to pay for it. "Delanie called you."

"She did," Ellie confirmed.

"Then you called Linc?"

His brother nodded. "Alex is babysitting."

"How is my niece?" Even as Sam asked about Leah, pain sliced through him as a picture of Phoebe's tear-streaked face flashed into his mind.

"She's fine."

Delanie walked over to the table. "What can I get you two?"

"Beer," Linc said.

"Club soda with lime," Ellie told her.

Sam met the bar owner's defiant gaze. "You're a blabbermouth. That could be bad for business."

"Depends on how you look at it. I take care of my customers. Folks appreciate that." The redhead shrugged. "I'll get those drinks for you."

"So." Sam met his sister's gaze. "No white wine? You're being a good example?"

"No. I'm pregnant." She looked at Linc before adding, "And yes, you're the last to know. I was going to make the announcement at the end of your wedding dinner."

"Congratulations." Sam put as much enthusiasm as possible into the single word. It wasn't much, though, what with envy choking off his goodwill. He wasn't proud of it. Especially the part where he was wallowing in self-pity.

"So, enough about me," she said. "Let's not waste time. You're a hot mess and it's because of Faith walking out."

"Don't sugarcoat it, sis. Tell me how you really feel."

"Okay. You're a quitter."

"Wow. That was supportive." He looked at Linc. "Want to jump in and back me up?"

"No. I agree with her."

Anger leaked through the alcohol buzz. And this was why he'd deliberately avoided family. "I'm surprised you didn't drag Cal away from work to pile on. So much for Team Sam."

Ellie was not discouraged. "You're giving up."

"Hold on." He pushed his empty beer glass away. "She left me."

"And now you're in a bar." Linc made it sound pathetic.

"You two are happily married. Not to each other. You know what I mean," Sam said. "When you're walking in my shoes, we'll talk."

"She is not Karen Leigh Perry." Ellie put her hand on his arm. "Faith is not the conniving bitch we all knew your wife was."

"Everyone knew?" Sam looked from his sister to his brother and both nodded. "Why didn't anyone tell me?"

"Would you have listened?" Ellie lifted one eyebrow. "Be honest."

He let out a sigh. "Doubtful."

"It's a family trait and not one of our better ones." There was sympathy in her expression now. "But I'm begging you to listen. Talk to Faith."

"I already did."

"Then do it again," she urged. "You have to fight for her."

"There's no point. She made her position clear."

"How?"

"She admitted she loves me and that's the problem." Before they could ask, Sam told them about her parents' emotional abandonment, then falling for her college sweetheart who'd claimed to love her. The last straw was when the guy walked out on her because she was pregnant with Phoebe.

"'Jerk' isn't a bad enough name for a loser like that." Ellie was seething with contempt.

"I could think of some." Linc's voice was low and menacing. "But they're not fit for mixed company, even if you are my sister."

"So you see," Sam continued, "I've got nothing to fight with."

His sister gave him a scolding look. "Like I said. Quitter."

"What do you want from me?"

"Don't throw in the towel. Be there. Show up everywhere. Get in her face. Actions speak louder than words. Let her know you're not going anywhere."

"Ellie, we lived together. I was there for her. It wasn't enough," Sam protested.

"Don't you see?" Her voice rose slightly in frustration. "By backing off you're playing into her hang-up. You're confirming that she's right to fear abandonment. Her parents ignored her. The jerk of a husband walked out on her and in her mind you're leaving her, too."

"Are you saying this is a test?" Sam dragged his fingers through his hair. "I was willing to marry her. She left me. At the altar."

"A technicality. And I don't think she's consciously testing you." Ellie waved her hand in dismissal. "She's been betrayed by love in a profound way and trust won't come easily."

Suddenly the light was beginning to penetrate his darkness. Sam got it.

"Take it from me," Linc said. "I never stopped loving

the woman I thought I divorced ten years ago. If Faith is it for you, don't roll on this. Unless you don't love her."

"I do. She knows it. I told her." And Sam couldn't believe he was telling them, that those words came out of his mouth. He was actually talking out loud about his feelings. Must be because a woman owned this bar.

"Okay, then," Ellie said. "If you want to be happy, you need to figure out a way to show her that you're not going anywhere."

"Wear her down," Sam clarified.

"Exactly," Ellie and Linc said together.

Sam didn't know about a third-date flower because he'd never needed one before. The plant lady had teased him about being the elusive Sam Hart. Not anymore. He was going to be gum on her shoe. Just let her try to get rid of him.

Chapter Fifteen

Faith and Phoebe were staying with Mayor Loretta Goodson-McKnight and her husband, Tom. The couple had married a couple years ago and moved into his house, which had three empty bedrooms since his kids were grown and gone. All of them were married now, too.

It had been a week since the aborted wedding and her hasty move out of Sam's house. She had worked her flower cart in the lobby of his building but tried to structure her hours for when there was the least chance of seeing him. The plan was a total bust. She'd had a Sam sighting every single day since that awful scene. He stopped to talk and always asked how she was, if Phoebe was doing all right and to let him know if there was anything she needed. He refused to go away.

What she needed was to get over missing him. Everything was different—no coffee together in the morning or being in his arms at night. But she had to put Phoebe first and make a new normal for her daughter. One without Sam.

After putting out the pink nightgown, she went into the family room where the child was curled up on Tom McKnight's lap. His wife was at a town council meeting and he had put on the movie *Frozen*, which Phoebe had seen about a million times. The more she looked at them, the more regret and guilt rushed through her.

She couldn't give her daughter a traditional family with a dad who'd be there for her. Faith felt like a colossal failure and the person she loved more than anything was paying the price. And now she had to be a mom to that person, the bad guy once again.

"Phoebe, it's time for bed."

There was no response. It was as if she hadn't said a word. Tom heard because he looked at her, then down at the little girl comfortably curled against him.

"Phoebe?" Faith said. "Did you hear me?"

"Uh-huh." But she didn't look over.

"You need to take a bath then we'll read."

"I don't want to."

Take a bath? Read? Or both? Since mutiny had been the go-to behavior for the past week, Faith figured it was number three. That produced more guilt because the kid probably felt as if everything in her life was out of her control. The least a mom could do was keep her child on a schedule so she could get the right amount of sleep and go to school ready to learn and grow up to be a productive member of society. Was that asking too much?

Fortunately none of that came out of her mouth, but she recognized that Phoebe was getting on her last nerve. It happened occasionally because she was a normal kid, but since they'd moved out of Sam's house she'd taken things to a whole new level of rebellion. Faith willed herself to patience and prayed it would hurry up.

"Phoebe, please turn off the movie."

The stern tone got a look. "But it's almost over."

"You can see the rest tomorrow."

"I want to see the end now." The hate stare from an eight-year-old was designed to burn straight to a mother's soul. It worked.

"You already know how it ends." *This is viewing number one million and one*, Faith thought, and she could recite it word for word.

Again the caustic words stayed in her head, thank goodness. But Tom must have felt the vibes. He met her gaze and there was understanding in his. He'd been a widower before marrying the mayor and had raised three kids by himself. To his credit, he stayed out of this mother/daughter standoff.

She and Phoebe were nose to nose—a line had been drawn in the sand. Her little girl was a seasoned negotiator and this was where there was normally pleading and puppy dog eyes. Tonight was different. There was open hostility and Faith felt the pressure of being between a rock and a hard place. If it was a weekend, there would be wiggle room, but school would start bright and early tomorrow.

Faith had to get tough. "Tom, I hate to do this, but would you turn off the movie, please?"

"No, Uncle Tom. Just a little more, please?" Phoebe turned the puppy dog eyes on him.

"Sorry, honey." He picked up the remote and did as requested. "Your mom outranks me."

"I don't know what that means," Phoebe grumbled.

"It means I make the rules," Faith said. "Say goodnight."

"Can I get a hug?" he asked.

Without protest the little girl reached her arms up and pressed her cheek to his chest. "'Night, Uncle Tom. I love you."

"Love you, too, honey. Sleep tight."

She scrambled off his lap and marched out of the room without even a hate stare for Faith. Tom gave her a sympathetic look before she followed her defiant daughter in order to supervise the bathing. It turned out to be fast and silent.

When her hair was dried and nightgown on, Phoebe climbed up on the twin bed and pulled the covers up, all by herself.

"Do you want to read to me or should I read to you?" Faith asked.

"Neither."

The snub rubbed a raw spot on Faith's feelings and she couldn't stop the words. "But this is what we always do."

"Nothing is like it was at Sam's."

This is what Faith had figured was at the core of the uprising. The good news was she didn't have to drag the information out of her. But there was bad news, too. Damage had been done. It was her duty as a mother to try to explain.

"Sweetie, I couldn't marry Sam." Faith clutched the book until her knuckles turned white.

"But why?" the little girl asked.

There were times when laying a guilt trip on a child was for the greater good, but this wasn't one of them. No way Faith would tell her that her loving Sam would hurt Phoebe in the long run.

"It just wouldn't have worked," she finally said. "Going through with the wedding would have hurt us all eventually."

"I don't believe you." The little girl sat up and stubbornly folded her arms over her chest. "I could have had a dad."

"Maybe for a little while. But in the end losing him would have been worse." Faith wasn't certain, but she had a sneaking suspicion that she was talking about her own feelings just then.

"You always tell me to at least try. But you didn't with Sam."

It wasn't like signing up for a soccer team or piano lessons. There were legalities and complex feelings involved. "This is different."

Phoebe shook her head. "Now everything is just ruined."

"It's not. You'll get over it." Again the words were for herself.

"No, I won't. And what you did is stupid."

"What have I said about calling people names, young lady?"

"I didn't say you were stupid." There was righteous passion in her child's eyes, the luxury of holding a viewpoint that put everything in black and white. "You love Sam and he loves you. Even a little kid can see that."

"It's not that simple."

"Yes, it is. But you ruined everything," she said again.

The words were like an arrow piercing her heart and drawing blood. It was the truth and Faith had no response. She was going to cry—ugly, blotchy, blubbery crying. And she didn't want her little girl to see it. Or anyone else for that matter.

"Okay then." She stood. "If you want to read your book, you can. You know what time to turn out the light." She bent and kissed her small cheek. "I love you. Sweet dreams."

Faith quickly turned away and walked into the hall, pulling the door half-closed behind her. She made it two more steps before burying her face in her hands. Silent sobs shook her shoulders for several moments, before she felt a strong arm come around her.

Without a word, Tom McKnight walked her into the family room and put her on the couch, then sat beside her. He got straight to the point. "Go see Sam."

The words snapped her out of it and she managed to stop crying. Through bleary eyes she met his gaze. "It's complicated."

"Because you're making it that way." He held up a finger when she started to protest. "Don't tell me I don't understand. Love is love whether you're sixteen or sixty. If you're lucky, the years give you wisdom, but sometimes a person's stubborn streak gets in the way."

"You're going to tell me an inspirational story now, right?" She took a shuddering breath and brushed at the moisture on her cheeks.

"Only you can decide whether or not it's inspiring." But the corners of his mouth curved up for a moment. "I fell in love with Loretta and wanted to marry her, but for reasons that seem silly now, I wanted my daughter settled down with a family, or at least in a relationship, before taking that step. Sydney knew it and pretended to be with Burke Holden so I could be happy."

"Pretended?" Faith said. "They're together now."

"Yeah. Funny thing about that pretending to be crazy about each other. It turned out to be real." He grinned. "The point is, I made things so difficult and complicated, my daughter felt she had to pull off a pretense to get me where I needed to be."

"I'm happy for you, Tom. And Loretta. She and my aunt Cathy were like sisters to each other and like mothers to me. But my situation is totally different. I have a little girl who absolutely must come first. I did what I thought was right, what was in her best interest." Her voice wavered then. "And I still ended up hurting her."

"Oh, honey—" He put his arm around her. "If anyone understands what hopeless feels like, it's me. When Syd's mom died in childbirth, I didn't think I could love anyone again. I was wrong. And you are, too. If you're happy, Phoebe will be. Trust me on that. It's the truth."

Maybe it was true before she walked out on the wedding and humiliated Sam in front of family and friends. But now? It was impossible to believe he still did and she loved him so much.

"I messed up big-time, Tom."

"Everyone does, honey. You're human."

"But there's no way to fix this. My daughter is going to hate me forever."

And Sam would, too.

It was quiet at Every Bloomin' Thing and almost time to close up shop. Faith was cleaning the long worktable in the back, tossing stems, leaves and scraps of ribbon from a large arrangement she'd deliver tomorrow. Catching sight of herself in the mirror on the wall, she winced. There was no way to sugarcoat the truth.

She looked like something the cat yakked up. The scene with Phoebe at bedtime last night just wouldn't go away and crying was her go-to response. And had been most of the night. Apparently the cold compress on her eyes hadn't worked because they were still puffy. In all fairness though, she couldn't blame the compress since that was external and her problem was on the inside. She was head over heels, madly in love with Sam Hart. But it was all over town that she'd left him at the altar.

Sam was a powerful, wealthy businessman who couldn't forgive such a public slap in the face. Heck, her own daughter was never going to forgive her and Phoebe wasn't powerful or wealthy. She was eight years old and really good at it.

Tears welled in her eyes for the billionth time, which would explain the chronic eye puffiness. She brushed away the wetness on her cheeks at the same time she heard the bell ring over the outer shop door, signaling a customer.

"Darn it. Now I have to be perky *and* puffy."

"Faith?" That was Sam's voice and there was a tone in it. He was worried. "Faith? Where are you?"

She rushed into the front and found him frantically looking around. "What's wrong, Sam?"

He rushed over and took her upper arms, holding her still, checking her out. "Are you all right?"

That was a very good question. Her heart was pounding, her knees were weak and it was hard to catch her breath. On top of that, her eyes were puffy. Otherwise she was fine.

"Faith—" He gripped her arms. "Answer me."

"What was the question?"

"Are you all right?"

She didn't get it. There was genuine concern leaning toward fear in his expression. "Don't I look all right?"

"Your eyes are a little red, but otherwise—"

"I'm fine, Sam. Why? You came rushing in here looking as if the place was on fire. What's going on?"

"That's what I'd like to know."

When he removed his hands from her arms, Faith was almost sure he did it reluctantly. As if maybe he didn't want to stop touching her any more than she wanted him to stop. But that was probably nothing more than wishful thinking.

"Why are you here?" she asked.

"Phoebe just called me and said you were in trouble."

And he'd come rushing to help her. Hold on, she thought. That didn't prove anything except he was good Blackwater Lake material and a caring neighbor. "As you can see, I'm fine. But my daughter has some explaining to do."

"So you're not in trouble?"

"No." At least not physically, she thought. "Thank you, Sam. I appreciate your concern, but there's nothing wrong. Except that my daughter is a manipulator. I'll make sure she doesn't bother you again."

"It was no bother." But something was bothering him because the hand he dragged through his hair was shaking.

Faith pulled the cell phone from her pocket and called McKnight Automotive. Tom had picked Phoebe up after school and was keeping her with him at the garage instead of dropping her off at the flower shop. He'd done it with his daughter, Sydney, when she was a little girl and said maybe Faith and Phoebe needed some space from each other.

The phone rang twice, then was picked up. "McKnight Automotive, Sydney speaking."

"Hi, Syd. This is Faith. May I speak to Phoebe, please?" *And give her a piece of my mind.*

"Sure, hold on. She's right here."

Faith heard voices on the other end, but not the conversation. It seemed to take longer than necessary for her daughter to come on the line. The little sneak.

Finally, she said, "Hello?"

"Hi, it's Mom."

"I know. Syd told me it was you."

"Do you know why I'm calling?" She glanced at Sam, who looked as if he was trying not to smile.

"To check on me?" There was a hopeful note in Phoebe's voice.

"Yes. Is everything all right?"

"Yup. I'm having fun with Uncle Tom and Syd. They're showing me stuff on cars."

"I'm glad to hear that." Faith knew if they were having this conversation face-to-face her little troublemaker would crumble like a sugar cookie. "Do you have anything else you want to tell me?"

There was a moment of silence, then she said, "I can't think of anything, Mommy."

"Have you talked to Sam recently?" This was it. The moment of truth. "It's not a hard question, Phoebe. Yes or no."

"Okay, then. Yes." A few seconds later she said, "He's there, isn't he?"

"You told him I was in trouble," Faith said sternly. "That's not true."

"It is, Mom. You said last night that losing him was bad. That means there's something wrong with you."

Wow, that was twisting the truth into a knot but Faith realized that the spirit of the message was valid. Although that's not what she was going to tell this child.

"Why would you do something like this?"

"Uncle Tom said it was for a good cause."

"He knew you called Sam?" Faith was shocked.

"It was his idea. He said somebody had to get the two of you together in the same room to have a talk. Do you want to ask him?" Phoebe said, trying to get off the hook.

"Not right now." But she would.

Several moments passed before the little girl said in an uncertain voice, "Mommy? Am I in trouble?"

"Are you in trouble?" she mused. Sam's expression indicated he was a no vote on that. "We'll talk about it when we get home."

"O-okay. Bye."

"Phoebe? I love you."

"Love you, too." She clicked off.

Faith let out a long breath and met Sam's gaze. "So we've been had by an eight-year-old and the brains of the operation is a grandfather who's old enough to know better."

"Tom McKnight?"

She nodded. "Or, as I will forever think of him now, Cupid. He thought we needed a push to talk to each other."

"I see." He slid his fingertips into the pockets of his worn jeans. "Are you going to discipline her?"

"There need to be consequences, Sam. She lied to you."

"But her intentions were good." He was taking Phoebe's side, just the opposite of excluding her. "And before you ground her for the rest of her life, you should know that I was already on my way here when she called me."

"It was a risky move on her part and might not have worked." Faith barely managed to get the words out, what with her heart pounding so hard.

"Why's that?" His gaze searched hers, questioning and intense.

"You had every right to ignore Phoebe and chalk it up to me getting what I deserved," she said. "I'm surprised you would be concerned about me at all after what I did."

"You don't get it yet." He was irritated, but somehow she knew it wasn't directed at her. "Faith, I'm not like your parents or that jerk of a husband who deserted you. I will always be there for you and Phoebe. Whether you want me to be or not."

Her heart squeezed tight and his words made her want to blubber like a baby. But she held it together. Hope blossomed inside her and it was important that she not blow this.

"Sam, I want you to know how sorry I am for leaving you at the altar."

"Technically it was an office, but—" He sighed. "It's all right—"

"Let me say it." She held up a hand to stop his words. "I might fumble this a little because groveling isn't what I'm known for. It's unnatural to me, but I'm willing to give it a try. For you."

"You have my undivided attention."

"I was wrong about love and you're the one who taught me that. You showed me your heart and it's as open and immeasurable as Big Sky Country. There's enough room for everyone you care about. No one gets left behind."

His eyes went soft, but no less intense. "No fumble there."

"I'm not finished yet." And thank goodness he was

still listening intently. "The thing is, I was afraid and that gives Phoebe a flawed message. That can't be the lesson she learns or she'll get love wrong, too. And I don't want that for her."

"You'll get no argument from me."

Good, but this was the tricky part. She walked over to her refrigerated case and pulled out two different-colored flowers, then came back to him. She handed him a lavender rose and a red one. "These are for love at first sight and forever-after love. I'm going out on a limb here, no pun intended because I'm a florist and work with plants. I'm asking you to forgive me and let me have a second chance. Marry me, please. Because I'm in love with you."

He nodded and the corners of his mouth curved up. "I'm going to have to think it over."

"What?" She blinked and her heart deflated like a punctured balloon. "Right. Of course. Because I should have—"

"Okay. Yes," he said.

"I'm sorry, what?"

"I thought it over. Actually, I've been thinking about you, nothing but you, since you walked out. And the answer is yes. There's nothing I want more than to marry you. Because I love you."

"Really?"

"Really. And I love your daughter. Let's get that straight right now." He looked at the roses, then pulled her into his arms. "I've never meant anything more. I would have said it first, but you took the words right out of my mouth. The I-love-you part, not the asking-for-forgiveness part. Because I didn't screw up."

"Are you ever going to let me live that down?"

"My current plan is to give Phoebe sisters and brothers and together we'll live happily ever after. But you should know that I might bring this up every twenty-five years or so."

"I love that plan," she said, smiling up at him. "So we should go to the courthouse for the wedding, take two—"

"No. Not a quickie courthouse thing." He was adamant. "I want a big splashy affair with you in an outrageously expensive and gorgeous white dress. Phoebe needs a fancy dress, too, because she's going to be the flower girl. No way we're sneaking off to do this quietly. Our love is a gift and should be celebrated and shared."

"That sounds like vows to me—" The tears started again, but they were all about joy this time.

"Please don't cry, sweetheart—"

"I'm just overwhelmed with happiness. You gave me shelter when I had nowhere to go and I never expected to find my future, too. The new guy in town is officially off the market."

He held her tighter and she knew home was and always would be in the shelter of his arms.

* * * * *

Looking for more
BACHELORS OF BLACKWATER LAKE?
Then keep an eye out for the next book in the series, available in November 2017!

And while you wait, catch up with residents of the picturesque Montana town:

JUST A LITTLE BIT MARRIED
A WORD WITH THE BACHELOR
HOW TO LAND HER LAWMAN
THE WIDOW'S BACHELOR BARGAIN
A DECENT PROPOSAL

Available now wherever Mills & Boon Cherish books and ebooks are sold!

When Charlotte Aldridge tells CEO Lucian Duval she's pregnant, the handsome billionaire is adamant his child will have the one thing he never did – the love of two committed parents…

Read on for a sneak preview of
THEIR BABY SURPRISE

'I want to be a part of this baby's life on a daily basis.'

The knot of anxiety inside her twisted. 'That's not possible, you know that, I'm moving away from London.'

'Don't move away.'

Charlotte gestured around her apartment. 'I need more space. I need to be near my parents. To have family close by.'

'I agree, that's why I believe you should move in with me…and for that matter, why we should marry.'

She sank down onto the window seat below the open window. 'Marry!'

'Yes.'

A known serial dater was proposing marriage. This was crazy. Lucian had the reputation for being impulsive and a maverick within the industry but his decisions were always backed up with sound logic. And that quick-fire decision making, some would even say recklessness, often gave him the edge over his more ponderous rivals. But he had called this one all wrong. She gave an incred-

P0617_1

ulous laugh. 'I bet you don't even believe in marriage?'

He rolled his shoulders and rubbed the back of his neck hard, his expression growing darker before he answered, 'It's the responsible thing to do when a child becomes part of the equation.'

This was crazy. She lifted her hands to her face in shock and exasperation, her hot cheeks burning against the skin of her palms. 'Have you really thought about what it takes to be a father? A child needs consistency, routine, to know that they are the centre of the parent's life. Have you considered the sacrifices needed? Your work life, the constant travel, all of the partying—everything about the way you live now will be affected. Are you prepared to give up all of that?'

Stood in the centre of the room, he folded his arms on his wide imposing chest, his eyes firing with impatient resolve. 'I don't have a choice. This child is my responsibility and duty, I will do whatever it takes to ensure that it has a safe and happy childhood.'